BOOK ONE OF THE
PEARCE STATION DUET

## Ann Grech

ISBN: 978-0-9954321-7-8
Edited by: Hot Tree Editing
Cover model: Gabriel Lapratte
Photographer: Paul Henry Serres
Cover design: Soxational Cover Art

*To all our Aussie farmers and station owners.*

# Blurb

Can the fresh-faced historian solve the legend of a gold-laden reef? Or will the seasoned station owner succeed in protecting his land at all costs?

Geeky graduate historian, Pete McKenzie, has spent seven years searching for Byron's fabled reef—the holy grail of gold deposits. Determined to be Australia's answer to Indiana Jones, a chance discovery sends Pete to outback Queensland, Pearce Station.

Forty-year-old station-owner, Scottie Pearce, calls outback Queensland home. The red dirt runs through his veins. But Scottie's protecting a secret that could destroy his family's five-generation legacy.

Fireworks blaze in this epic tale of lust, love, and betrayal as both men discover a treasure they weren't even searching for... outback treasure.

**Outback Treasure I is the first part of the Pearce Station duet. Pete and Scottie's story concludes in Outback Treasure II, releasing on 18 May 2020.**

# Acknowledgements

The inspiration for this story came from an episode of Josh Gates' Expedition Unknown. In that episode, he spoke about the legend of a lost reef of quartz, littered with gold nuggets in the Aussie outback. Byron's story is based on a true to life person, but all the names have been changed to protect Byron's living relatives. Thank you for the inspiration, Mr Gates!

A huge thank you to Robyn and Simon Corcoran, Luke Newton and Kaitlin Bryant. Your advice on Pearce Station, and everything associated with it, made up for this suburban girl's lack of knowledge. It's a whole lot more realistic than it was before your input, and I greatly appreciate that. Any errors or artistic licence I've taken are my own!

Sharon Hayes, I appreciate you reviewing the story from the perspective of our Indigenous Australians. It was important to me to properly honour our indigenous cultural heritage, so thank you.

Lisa (LJ) Harris and Kariss Stone, your feedback on the draft of this story was also very much appreciated. Chapter 1 is in much better shape now!

My beautiful friends who make up the MM DreaMMers authors (Viva Gold, LJ Harris, JJ Harper, Angelique Jurd, Tracy McKay, Megs Pritchard, and JP Sayle), thank you for your advice, inspiration, daily pics and keeping me motivated. You ladies are amazing. I'm grateful every day for your friendship.

To the team at Hot Tree Editing, thank you. Becky, my gorgeous editor and advisor, I couldn't do this without your cheerleading. I loved your comments in the spine, and I'm so glad you adored these boys.

Gabriel and Paul Henry, thank you for the magic you created in front of and behind the lens in bringing my exact vision of Scottie to life. Tracey Weston from Soxational Cover Art, you've brought Pearce Station to life in vivid colour and combined with the gorgeous photo, it's stunning. I adore the artwork that you've put together for this duet.

Linda Russell from Foreward PR, this is the first time we're working together. Cheers to many more! Thank you for all the work you've done behind the scenes to get these boys out into the world. It's truly appreciated.

To my hubby and kiddos, I couldn't do this without your support, although a few less dirty socks on the floor would make life a lot easier! I love you all to the moon and back.

Last and most certainly not least, thank you to you, the readers and bloggers, for your unending love and support. Sharing, reviews, general shout outs and, importantly, reading our words means the world to every author. This is my eleventh novel. It's something I never dreamed possible, but you've made that a reality for me. For that – the realization of a childhood dream – I'll forever be grateful.

Ann xx

# Glossary

This story is set in outback Queensland, Australia. It uses Australian English. There are some terms that you might not have heard before, so I have set out a few for you. If you come across more, please let me know and I'll try to explain our slang. You might also want to take a peek at my website too – I'll add more there as they come up.

**Akubra** – a broad brimmed hat.

**Autumn** – fall.

**Ballsed it up** – screwed it up.

**Barbie** – short for barbecue, but in this context it's a grill, not a smoker.

**Billy** – tea pot.

**Biscuits** – cookies.

**Bloke** – man.

**Bonza** – great, awesome.

**Brekkie** – breakfast.

**Brick shithouse** – an outhouse made of bricks (much more upmarket than your standard corrugated iron shitter).

**Brissie** – Brisbane. Queensland's capital city and location of the Ekka.

**Buggered** – screwed, broken.

**Bundy** – Bundaberg Rum.

**Bushells** – a brand of tea (the drink, not the dinner kind!).

**Carnarvon** – a town in Western Australia.

**Carnarvon Gorge** – a national park (bushland) in Queensland, on the east coast of Australia.

**Centimetres** – metric unit of measurement. One inch equals 2.54 centimetres.

**Chips** – French fries.

**Chook** – chicken.

**Clip you** – hit you.

**CSIRO** - Commonwealth Scientific and Industrial Research Organization, a government organization responsible for scientific research aimed at improving the performance of industry to enhance economic and social performance for the benefit of the entire country.

**Dagwood dogs** – a sausage on a stick, dipped in batter and deep fried.

**Damper** – a form of bread traditionally baked in the embers of an open fire.

Dogger – a hunter of feral dogs and dingo cross breeds.

**Drizabone** – a jacket designed to be worn by horse riders.

**Dunny** – toilet.

**Ekka** – a nickname for Royal Queensland Show originally called Brisbane Exhibition (Ekka is short for exhibition). It is an annual agricultural fair in Queensland.

**Fair dinkum** – for real, seriously.

**Fairy floss** – cotton candy.

**Fella** – bloke, man.

**Flannie** – a flannel button down shirt.

**Footie** – rugby league, a full contact sport played between two teams for two forty minute halves where the objective is to score more than the other team by carrying the ball over the 'try line' and, after making a try, kicking the ball between the posts to add an extra two points to the score (called a conversion).

**G'day** – hello.

**Hack it** – handle it.

**Helluva** – hell of a.

**Hullabaloo** – noise.

**IGA** – a supermarket chain of independent grocers.

**Jam** – jelly.

**Jocks** – underwear.

**Jumper** – sweater.

**Kalgoorlie** – a town in southern outback Western Australia.

**Kitchen bench** – kitchen countertop.

**Ks** – short for kilometres, a metric unit of measurement. One mile is the equivalent of 1.6 kilometres.

**Longreach** – a town in outback Queensland.

**Lost my shit** – become upset or agitated.

**Mardi Gras** – the Sydney Gay and Lesbian Mardi Gras.

**Metre** – a metric unit of measurement. One hundred centimetres equals one metre, which is approximately three feet.

**Milo** – a chocolate powder that you can drink warm or cold in milk, or on ice cream as a dessert.

**Mobile phone** – cell phone.

**Never Never** – outback Australia.

**Nicked off** – left, departed.

**Noggin'** – head.

**Outhouse** – an outdoor dunny. Also called a shitter or toilet.

**Paddock** – a corral for livestock.

**Pastoral lease (of Pearce Station)** – a long-term lease granted over state-owned land to a person for the agricultural purposes such as agistment and cattle grazing. Where 'exclusive possession' is not a term of the lease (as is the case with Pearce Station), others may traverse the land, such as those who hold permits under the *Mineral Resources Act 1989* (Qld) or the indigenous custodians who have recognized 'native title' rights. Native title was a phrase coined by the High Court of Australia in its historic abolition of *terra nullius* a Latin term forming part of international law at Australia's settlement (the case is *Mabo v Queensland (No 2)* [1992] HCA 23, (1992) 175 CLR 1 (3 June 1992)). *Terra nullius* means 'nobody's land', which justified the importation of British law and customs into Australia, purportedly overriding indigenous custodians' traditions and laws and dispossessing them of the land, and rendering indigenous custodians as 'non-citizens'. The abolition of *terra nullius* by Australia's highest court allowed recognition of the continuing underlying land rights of indigenous Australians where certain conditions were met. Native title allows rights of access, camping or living on areas, visiting and protecting important places, hunting, fishing, gathering from the land, taking of traditional resources (for example water, wood, stone, ocre), conducting social, cultural, religious activities on-site, and the teaching of traditional customs and laws.

**Piss weak** – pathetic.

**PJs** – pyjamas.

**Pollie** – politician.

**Poofter** – a slur for gay men, equivalent to faggot.

**Postie** – postal worker.

**Prospecting permit** – a permit granted under the *Mineral Resources Act 1989* (Qld) which allows for fossicking of minerals, including gold, using handheld implements.

**Pulling my leg** – joking.

**Queenslander** – a style of architecture for houses built in Queensland to suit the varied climate in the state (sub-tropical to desert). Traditionally, the houses are constructed on stilts to allow for ventilation and flood waters to pass under the house, with wide verandas and windows all around the house. Painted in a light colour, the combination ensures cooling shade and cross ventilation.

**Ranga** – red headed person.

**Rip-roaring** – high in intensity.

**Rocky or Rockhampton** – a regional city in Queensland.

**Roo** – kangaroo.

**Rubbish** – trash.

**Sanga** – sandwich.

**Scoffed** – ate.

**Scone** – a sweet biscuit (i.e. American-style biscuit, not a cookie) that you traditionally eat with jam (i.e. jelly) and whipped cream.

**Servo** – gas station.

**Sheila** – woman.

**Shit a brick** – panicked, freaked out.

**Shopping centre** – mall.

**Sick as dogs** – very unwell.

**Supermarket** – grocery store.

**State of Origin** – rugby match between the mighty Queensland Maroons (the Cane Toads) and the meh at best New South Wales Blues (the Cockroaches). Usually the Blues have the blues because even though the stubborn bastards will never admit it, Queensland is by far the better team. Go Queenslander!

**Station** – equivalent to a ranch.

**Swag** – a canvas sleeping bag.

**Tap** – faucet.

**Tea** – depending on the context, either a hot beverage or dinner.

**Tele** – television.

**The Alice or Alice Springs** – a town in the Northern Territory, in the heart of central Australia.

**Trackies** – sweats.

**Truckies** – truck drivers.

**Tucker** – food.

**Undies** – underwear.

**Uni** – university.

**Ute** – equivalent to a pickup truck.

**Veggie patch** – vegetable garden.

**Yobbo** – a loud and obnoxious Australian, usually a bloke.

**Yonder** – out there (a non-specific description of somewhere not close).

# THE PLAYERS – BYRON'S TIME

**Winston Able** – the dingo hunter (scalper) who joined the expedition for Byron's gold much later than the others. He was brought in as somewhat of a babysitter when the expedition started to fall apart.

**John Blackwood** – the expedition leader. He was highly experienced in the outback, having traversed central Australia numerous times on a bicycle and on foot; however, never with a team and certainly not with heavy machinery. He was not a fan of Byron's.

**Errol H Byron** – the man who alleged to have found a quartz reef in outback Australia laden with gold. He was the subject of Pete's fascination.

**Harry Cooper** – pilot of the expedition plane, a Gipsy Moth aptly named the *Spirit of Gold*.

**Dick Katter** – the infamous union boss who funded Byron's expedition by persuading labour union members to invest in it. He was the founder of the Centralian Gold Prospecting Organization (or the CGPO) and ultimately the person who Byron, and Blackwood, had to report to.

# Prologue

## February 1930, Sydney

## – Errol H. Byron

The biting cold wind howled, and the rain came down in sheets, pooling along the narrow streets of the docklands. My umbrella and trench coat provided me some protection, but the thick fabric of my trousers was drenched and stuck to my shins, nevertheless. Beggars lined the streets, huddling under awnings and fruitlessly searching for a stray penny. The more respectable ones scrounged for paid work, doing anything to earn a coin and feed their offspring. The streets were usually grimy and gritty, the smell of burning coal and rotting fish in the air, but the rain had washed most of it away, bringing with it a freshness alongside the chill.

Despite the lack of stench, factories down by the wharf were no place for genteel folk. My wife, bless her, was at home raising our twins, Betty and Bobby. But me? I was street smart and on a mission. I looked to the east between the red brick buildings to the harbour. Crystalline blue on a good day and brown and murky on a less than perfect one like today, the harbour was Sydney's lifeline. A key to its wealth.

But my focus was the other direction.

Inland. Into the Never Never.

Hard times had befallen our lucky country. The 1929 stock market crash had driven the world into a deep depression—the worst in history. I made my own luck, never reliant on others to provide me with an opportunity. However, I wasn't unaffected. The bailiff sought payment of the debts I accrued during my months toiling on the original design of the Sydney Harbour Bridge. But the blueprints were stolen from me and payment went to another. The man was a charlatan, not an engineer. My generosity with my expertise—my attempts to assist him and share the wealth of my knowledge—had been my downfall. But it would not be the end of me. I would not only survive but succeed, a testament to my vast skills. I was a highly competent surveyor and pro-spector, an inventor too.

I had something even more significant to of-fer than a national building project such as the Har-bour Bridge or my inventions. This country needed a saviour: me. The Australian government was in its in-fancy and I held no confidence in it. The Member for Kalgoorlie had already foolishly refused my offer, but I would not be deterred. In fact, I was pleased. Work-ing with the government would have unnecessarily curbed my ability to control the expedition—some-thing I would not compromise on. I would see to its success. My setbacks had built character, but I'd been educated on the ways of the corrupt and the imprudent. I had always been immensely intelligent, and now I was wiser too.

My intelligence and renown among Sydney's elite had men in society's highest echelons seeking to meet with me. Word had gotten out about my intention to recover my find, and I was about to meet with the most influential of all Sydney's men. Dick Katter was infamous, commanding both his union members' loyalty and the ears of the new government. He wielded that power to promote interests that really mattered. Like my offer. For a worthwhile investment, he could join with me and we would reap the rewards of not only a once in a lifetime opportunity, but perhaps the single greatest opportunity for our fair country. I would be its hero.

My destination: central Australia. An expedition over thousands of miles through the very centre of our red continent. A difficult trek for even the most hardened. But the returns would be immediate.

What is it that I was offering you may ask?

Gold.

In concentrations and of a purity the likes of which had never been seen before. A quartz reef with colours ranging from rust through to the purest of whites, with nuggets of gold littered among the stone. Its recovery would prove easy, and my plan was foolproof.

And that gold would make us all rich beyond our wildest imaginations.

# ONE

---

## Present day, Sydney

## – Pete

Papers were strewn across the table in front of me. My tablet sat to my right, my coffee to the left. One corner of the black, red, and white poster I had tacked to the wall fluttered in the breeze from the heater. The words were supposed to inspire me. "When people ask you, 'What do you do?' Tell them, 'Whatever it takes.'" Sometimes they were frustrating as hell. Like now. Because my quest to find Australia's El Dorado was withering. Good things were never supposed to be easy. Success was a measure of a man's persistence. I'd had all types of motivational posters up around the place at one time or another, much to my landlord and flatmate's dismay. But my persistence was wearing thin, and I was sick of the good things never materializing. I'd hit a brick wall, and I was getting nowhere. It wasn't the first time I was reconsidering the wisdom of my obsession.

I usually plugged on, but I was at my wits' end. I needed a win. Something. Anything.

But it was no use. Something wasn't right. It wasn't adding up. Or maybe it was, and I'd been suckered into the search for Errol H Byron's fabled gold and it just didn't exist.

I'd read all the accounts. I knew he was a crazy bastard. He was probably lying when, right in the middle of the Great Depression, he bragged of finding a quartz reef laden with gold in the outback. But I didn't doubt that it existed. Just that he wasn't being entirely truthful with his expedition party about where it was located. The accounts of that ill-conceived crusade into the outback made Byron out to be more than a little paranoid and mostly insane. But I thought everyone had missed an important detail. He was stealthy. Incredibly secretive. And my gut feeling was that he deceived everyone—or nearly everyone.

Byron, for all his faults, was a storyteller. He held an audience captivated. With as big a personality as Western Australia and an unmistakable air of confidence and mystery, he managed to talk a hardened union boss into investing thousands of pounds into what was ultimately a wild goose chase. With the influential Katter throwing his weight behind Byron's fanciful story, Byron managed to get an expedition party kitted out at short notice with the best that technology had on offer.

The front door opening made me jump. My flatmate, and landlord, usually worked late, but when I glanced at the clock on the oven, I grimaced at how late he actually was. "Working hard?" he asked as he let the door close behind him with a soft thud. Surveying the seemingly chaotic mess I worked in, he shook his head.

"Always." I yawned. "But I've hit a brick wall." I picked up the stylus lying next to my tablet and spun it in my fingers. "I've got nothing." I tapped the pen-like instrument against the white tabletop in frustration, resisting the urge to throw it. "How was work?"

He shook his head. "Don't ask." He groaned and let his head fall back. "Shitty day." He looked exhausted. He wore a suit and tie to work, made excellent money and was apparently successful by every measure of adulthood. Something I was yet to achieve. But, truthfully, aside from knowing he was a lawyer, I had no idea what he did for a living. He was pretty senior despite his age. I'd heard him talking about strata law, duties of care and disclosure before, but he tended to deflect when I asked him about work, just like he did then. Whoever he acted for, he was perpetually stressed out and tired. I wondered if it was worth it. It wasn't like he was living the high life, dating beautiful women, driving fancy cars. With the exception of his current girlfriend of three months, he'd been single for the four years that I'd lived with him and he took the bus to work. He didn't even own a car.

Phoenix tugged off his tie and unbuttoned the top few buttons of his shirt before plucking a bottle of beer from his shelf on the fridge. Unlike me, Phoenix not only had all five of the food groups represented in his kitchen supplies, he had beer. I lived on the basic diet of a poor student most of the time—noodles, vegemite sandwiches, and coffee. He kept me around because I paid rent and made his life interesting with my random historical facts. Truthfully, though, he'd probably have been better off with a cat.

"Go back to the beginning then. Walk me through it." He twisted open the Corona, popped a wedge of lemon in it and leaned back against the kitchen bench, his legs crossed at his ankles waiting expectantly.

I sighed and rubbed my eyes. Grateful to be able to talk through my predicament, I did what he suggested and started at the beginning. "Okay, so you know my theory. Cooper, the pilot assigned to Byron's expedition, was always mentioned as an aside." His plane, the *Spirit of Gold,* was a Gipsy Moth. Small, light and high tech for the times. It didn't need a long runway, but it didn't have the fuel range that modern aircraft did, which meant carrying fuel for it, or pre-arranging drops.

"Yep." He took a swig, draining half the bottle in one go. "No one wanted Cooper and his plane there except Byron. You think that their importance has been underestimated." He recited my own lines back to me, ones I'd told him more than once. It was frustrating knowing how little progress I'd made in recent months after spending years narrowing down the possible locations of the reef.

"Exactly." I nodded before leaning my head against the backrest on the uncomfortable, but stylish, chair. "In all my readings of Byron, he was depicted as paranoid and secretive. He fed the other team members just enough information to keep them champing at the bit, but never revealed enough to give them any real power." He kept the reef's location a secret for the entire trip.

"Right," Phoenix added. "The expedition fell apart and they all went their separate ways. Byron gets the freedom he needs to travel to the reef without everyone else there, but he's still got the resources of—what was the gold company's name—anyway, them at his disposal."

"Yeah, the Centralian Gold Prospecting Organization. They invested thousands of pounds of members' money at the height of the Great Depression."

I'd been learning about Byron for seven years, ever since my first semester at uni. Our lecturer for my modern Australian history course had started speaking about some of the myths of the age when she'd mentioned Byron. At first, I'd felt sorry for his first wife, who he disappeared on, and then I'd heard about his second and the kids they'd had together. His kids had grown up knowing their father was a bigamist and had tricked a nation into giving more than it could afford to lose at a time in history when every penny was hard to come by. My intentions had been honourable in that first assignment—prove that Byron wasn't as bad as everyone said he was so that his wives and kids could have some of their dignity restored.

It hadn't happened.

The more I dug, the more invested in his story I became. The more I was afflicted with gold fever. In the years since, I'd scoured maps, read every piece of information I could lay my hands on and reached what could be my own fanciful conclusion. Byron had intended that the expedition would fall apart. He'd led them all on a wild goose chase, extending the expedition by months. They'd travelled into the harshest of climates and terrains. I didn't have any hard evidence, but I think it was all intentional. Summer was like an inferno in the outback. It wasn't a time to be prospecting for gold. The heat was so intense that a human could bake to death in mere hours without water. The heat so thick it was visible—the shimmer it created off the land morphed the red dirt with the deepest of blue skies, making the horizon all but invisible. The sun would have beaten down on the spinifex and iron-hard mulga trees and created a perfect storm of misery, hopelessness, and anger. At the time, Australia was in the grips of a years-long drought too, much as it currently was, and the travellers were going into some of the driest landscapes in the world. And yet, the expedition headed off in spring. There was only a small window of opportunity to find the reef. Wasting time wasn't in anyone's interest.

I continued on. "My guess is that he kept the reef's true location secret. He made sure he could get there and back quickly, and had a strategy to haul out some of the heavy gold with minimal witnesses, and fewer people to share it with."

"So, send the expedition off in the wrong direction?" Phoenix asked. But it wasn't really a question. He knew my thoughts on what Byron was capable of. "You've said it before, but could he have been that cruel? It seems excessive, especially when he was on the expedition too."

I raised my shoulders in a shrug. "It does, but I can't dismiss the possibility at this point." Was he that conniving? Could Byron have played his part so well that the expedition didn't suspect they were being double-crossed? Had he managed to plant the seeds of distrust between the expedition members and through his eccentric behaviour and secrecy and forced them to lose hope? It did seem far-fetched, but could it have been strategic? "If Byron knew the actual location of the reef—and evidence suggests it was fake—but if he did, like I said, the only person Byron needed was the pilot and his airplane. At least for a quick snatch and grab anyway. Cooper was the only person on the expedition who Byron was keen to have on board. It couldn't have been a coincidence. They just needed to haul enough gold for the two of them to disappear and live their lives in comfort." It would certainly have been much less than the Centralian Gold Prospecting Organization would have wanted after its hefty investment. I sighed, frustration bubbling over. Giving up on this was easy. All I had to do was turn my back and get on with my life. But I was too damned stubborn to do that. "I don't know. It's all specula- tion, but my gut's telling me that the whole expedition reeked of something fishy." There were too many accounts of gold discoveries in the far reaches of the outback for the story of the reef to be entirely made up. No-one had found it yet, but that didn't mean it didn't exist.

"Okay, so you're convinced that it exists. Where is it?"

"That's the million-dollar question, isn't it? I've got no idea." I groaned and stretched. My arse was asleep, and my feet had pins and needles. "I feel like I'm this close—" I pinched my thumb and forefinger together "—to finding it, but in reality, I'm in exactly the same place I was six months ago." I paused. "Nope, I've backtracked. Because now I've completely ruled every square kilometre of search area out."

"Maybe it's time then, Pete." He smiled sympathetically at me. "I know you don't want to hear it, but maybe your parents and sister have a point. You've been chasing this for years and you're no closer than you were when you started out." He downed the rest of the beer and tossed the bottle into the recycling bin, the glass clinking against the others in there, before he clapped me on the shoulder and wandered into his bedroom.

"Yeah, maybe," I muttered, not having any intention of walking away. My gut was still telling me it was out there. I'd followed it every other time. There was no way I was going to stop doing it now when, even though I'd gotten nowhere, it felt like I was so close to another breakthrough.

My parents thought I was delusional. Frustrated with me, they just wanted me to do something productive with my life. Apparently two degrees and becoming Australia's expert on Byron wasn't it. My sister said I was an embarrassment for chasing something so ridiculous and refused to even speak to me about it. The fact that her latent homophobia pinged every time I got near didn't help either. Their disapproval had been weighing heavily on me lately, but I'd promised myself that I wouldn't give up until I had an answer. At this point, it was sheer obstinacy and the desire to prove my family wrong that motivated me to sit at that table.

I rubbed my eyes again and groaned as my muscles screamed from sitting in the same hunched-over position for hours. As if I'd summoned them with my thoughts, an email notification pinged on my screen from Mum. I needed the distraction, so I clicked on it.

I shouldn't have.

*Peter,*

*You would be perfect for some of these jobs. You could be a lab tech in the geology department in a uni in the country. There's even a position doing history research in Hobart. You should apply. Please apply. You need to put this silly obsession out of your mind. You've spent years looking for it. It doesn't exist. You know that. We only want what's best for you, you know that.*

*I'll call you soon.*

*Mum*

She meant well, she really did. But she and Dad were great at reducing my years of work into a flippant dismissal. She had a point though—how long was I going to keep following the trail? Now that I'd finished my latest degree, I really had no excuse to put off finding a job. A real one, not the one that I'd managed to hold down for the last few months. They just wanted what was best for me; they didn't understand that my goals were different from theirs. I'd graduated two days earlier, and the topic of conversation over our celebratory lunch had quickly turned to what I had planned. No doubt it's what prompted Mum's email. When I'd muttered that I was going to find Byron's gold, Mum had sighed, and Dad became impatient. My sister rolled her eyes like she was apt to do because my plans hadn't involved settling down and becoming an adult. They figured at age twenty-five, I should have my future figured out, rather than still be chasing a myth. I may have been the resident expert on Byron, but what it really meant was that I was an underemployed graduate with degrees in history and extractive mining. I struggled to pay rent in the most expensive city in Australia, my family were unimpressed, and I was still obsessed.

Rescuing the email from my deleted items and looking at the jobs didn't sound too bad. Or maybe I just needed a break. Phoenix would be in bed in a few minutes so he wouldn't want to go out. I debated for all of a moment before picking up the phone and dialling one of the few people that at a stretch I'd call a friend from uni. "Hey, Kath."

"Hi, Pete," she replied. She sounded distracted and there was a hell of a lot of noise in the background. "What's up?"

"You guys up to anything?" I asked hopefully. "You maybe wanna go out for a coffee?"

"We're at a club," she said, laughing. Drunken cheers sounded in the background. "Come out with us."

Yeah, no. The clubs they went to weren't even close to my scene. Gay bar? Maybe. But I wasn't in the right frame of mind to hook up. "Sure, I might see you there." We said goodbye and it didn't escape my notice that she hadn't told me which club they were at and I hadn't asked. This was why I preferred the company of books and legend.

But all my books still hadn't helped me find the reef. It didn't narrow down my search area to anything less than the whole of the sprawling central region of Australia. The scale of the landscape was something a city slicker like me couldn't imagine. It held a certain romance even though it was deadly. The never-ending skies were unbroken by high-rise towers and pollution and the red sandy dirt that defined the heart and soul of the outback stretched out underfoot. The wild, scrubby bushland that was uniquely Australian represented her people so well—they were a little wild themselves. I couldn't help but get caught up in admiration for the sheer strength of will possessed by the early pioneers who were gutsy enough to venture out into the Never Never, conquering it and surviving the desert crossing. Even Byron, who I held the least respect for from those involved in his expedition, still deserved his dues for making the trek.

I spun the stylus in my hand and sighed in frustration. What wasn't I seeing? I'd poured over every square inch of digital map of the Northern Territory looking for Byron's reef. Finding it was never going to be easy. I was searching for a proverbial needle in a haystack and his instructions were far from clear: head west from Alice Springs. That was it. My passion had always been history. Pouring over maps and historical notes of expeditions long forgotten, deciphering hand-drawn maps and rediscovering the magic of the land and its people. It was wild country out there. Dry, hot, harsh. Deadly. I couldn't wait to narrow down the search area and leave the city to go in search of it. Something in me yearned to go on an adventure. To get my hands dirty.

But there was no reef. I, like everyone before me, was looking in the wrong spot. That damn reef had become the stuff of legend. Australia's very own holy grail. And, damn it, I was Indiana Jones. I *was* going to find it.

My eyes were gritty from the bad fluorescent lighting overhead, and my stomach rumbled. My half-arsed dinner was long since forgotten. I took a swig of my coffee and grunted my objection. It was stone cold. I needed to stretch my legs. I'd been at it for hours and made no progress. Again. It was easy to get lost in history. In legend.

Knees creaking, I got up to hit start on the coffee machine and rummaged through my shelf in the fridge for leftovers. The only thing in there was lunch meat, which still smelled fresh enough. The two-day-old bread wasn't mouldy yet, so I slapped my pre-midnight snack together and munched down as the pod finished dripping into my mug. I wet my face and looked over to the mess strewn all over the table in disdain. It was no longer even remotely organized.

Then I saw it. The map of Australia. The ranges which, from my perspective, were to the left of Alice Springs—in Queensland. Could it be that simple? Could Byron have sent the expedition out west of Alice Springs, but actually meant east? The land there bordered the Great Artesian Basin and there was, no doubt, gold in the region. With a couple of refuelling stops, Cooper's plane could have travelled that far. He'd made the trip from Sydney to the Alice before. The flight to western Queensland would have required half as many refuelling stops. Could that really be it? Surely it wasn't that simple.

Byron had described his desert meanderings as having begun from Carnarvon. But the coordinates he gave put them somewhere in the Indian Ocean. Right from the word go, Byron had lied. What if he was referring to another Carnarvon? I was sure there was another. My sandwich landed on the bench where I tossed it haphazardly and my coffee cup lay untouched at the machine as I raced back to the table to check the maps again.

My heart slammed against my chest, racing as anticipation overtook me. Was this where Cooper and Byron had gone after they'd reunited, found the reef and disappeared. Every expedition—organized or not—had scoured the area west of Alice Springs. But no one as far as I knew had looked east.

It seemed a little too coincidental that there would be two places named Carnarvon, but my search revealed that there was, in fact, one in Queensland, on the opposite side of the country to Western Australia. Could the reef be between the Alice and Queensland's Carnarvon Gorge instead of where every bloke and their dog, and of course I, had been looking?

Google Earth was working overtime in a matter of seconds while I brought up the three locales. My fingers shook as I watched the page load, my brow breaking out in a sweat. The two Carnarvons were separated by the distance of the entire continent—three and a half thousand Ks. But draw a line horizontally across the three, and they were barely two hundred kilometres apart.

I let that sink in. Three plot points on a map. In a near straight line.

There was no way the two Carnarvons could be mixed up, but maybe the mention of Carnarvon had slipped. Maybe Byron hadn't intended to reveal it, but in his wild storytelling, he'd gotten carried away. Had Byron left a breadcrumb without even realizing what he was doing? There was only one way to know for sure. I bit back a yawn and started the long process of checking every inch of map to the east of the Alice.

The clang of metal hitting metal sounded behind me, and I jumped, startling awake. I stretched my neck, trying to rid the crick in it from falling asleep at the table. Again. I'd been pouring over maps of western Queensland every spare minute for the last three weeks. Unsurprisingly, there was nothing. I was losing hope again. My supposed break-through was nothing more than a far-fetched theory. As fanciful a tale as Byron's claim to have located the mythical reef.

I blinked away the exhaustion I carried like a second skin these days and looked at my tablet. It'd gone flat, probably hours ago, so I plugged it in, made another coffee, and psyched myself up for a few more hours of searching before I had to put on my penguin suit and go to my actual job as a hotel bell boy.

The clang sounded again, and I looked around, moving over to the window overlooking the construction site next door. A pile driver was ramming metal poles into the ground, preparing for the new high-rise building that was being built. My head throbbed with each bang and my eyes were dry and itchy. I groaned. It was going to be a long few hours.

Getting comfortable on the kitchen table chair, I pulled one foot up underneath me and took a fortifying sip of the steaming brew. As much as I would deny taking after my parents and their love for an overly extravagant lifestyle, coffee was the one thing I wouldn't compromise on. I needed good coffee. I liked my coffee like my men—strong and hot.

With the dull slamming of the pile driver rattling in my brain, I moved the map an inch and continued combing the screen for any sign of rock formations. On and on I moved the map, fastidiously checking and double-checking before shifting it.

Then I saw it.

Lighter red than the rest of the area with some patches of white interspersed through the uneven surface. Lots of grass and underbrush, but the white rocks were unmistakable. The image looked as if it shimmered. The heat radiating from the ground when the satellite image was taken made even the clearest of images appear like it moved. I zoomed in again, narrowing my focus down onto the small patch of outback dirt. As the image refreshed and cleared, I held my breath. Then I zoomed in again. The pixelated image focussed in a smooth transition down the screen and I muttered a stunned, "Fuck me."

It was right there in front of me. An outcropping of what could easily be quartz. Some parts were a dusty red and others a purer white. The short, bushy foliage of the invincible acacia shrub bushes dotted throughout were a faded blue-grey against the rich red soil. Australia's red heart right there in front of me. The picture on the screen before me was stunning. Untouched and raw. The rich colours were so vibrant that I instinctively touched the screen to check what I was seeing was real. It was breathtakingly beautiful. I blinked, trying to regather my scattered thoughts. Analysis. That's what I was doing. But before I hotfooted to the outback to find Byron's lost gold, I had to verify more details. Size, topography, ownership of the land, permits, and buying an off-road four-wheel drive. I mentally put the brakes on. Any expedition would be no overnight project.

So first, verification. I followed the line of the scar in the land and marked out its boundaries. With every move of the map onscreen, my excitement grew. It was huge. Kilometres long and wide too. When it was fully mapped, I zoomed out again to see what was before me.

A jagged scar torn through the land like the claw mark of a big cat.

My heart crashed against my chest, beating in a wild rhythm. Excitement bloomed. It was a close enough match to Byron's estimate. Years of looking. Of searching. Of reading and plotting out routes, deciphering and decoding messages that might not have even been in communications. Of sorting through the speculation and grand posturing of Byron himself and the self-preservation-motivated retellings of others on the expedition and others since then. And finally, I'd found something. Nothing I'd ever located before had come close.

Could I have really stumbled across it? Was this rock formation Byron's fabled reef? I'd always believed that the find was fortuitous but that I could find it again with meticulous research. But deep in the recesses of my mind, I'd wondered. I'd pondered whether it was out there just waiting to be stumbled on again. Whether it would only reveal itself to a lucky few. Could I be that lucky one?

The cogs in my brain turned to more immediate questions—who owned the land now? Could I get access? Did I have enough data for a prospecting permit? By now I was familiar enough with the region. It didn't take me long to find the land on maps and figure out its name and address.

Pearce Station. A cattle station a good few hours out of Longreach. The station itself was on a scale I couldn't fathom—five thousand square kilometres. Bigger than New York with enough left to spare that just under half of Los Angeles would fit in it too. One owner.

I wondered what that owner would say to my application for the prospecting permit, which gave me access rights to their lease. Was he some gnarled old man, hardened and weathered like the outback he lived in? He probably wouldn't appreciate some city slicker traipsing all over his station. I looked at the land again. Not the rock formation, but the homestead and the sheds surrounding it.

The deep red of the dirt and the blue-grey vegetation. I wondered whether the rugged hills in the distance would look almost purple. I closed my eyes and found myself there, staring in wonder at the station and its people. I couldn't make out any of them, but I knew that I was meant to find this place. That I was meant to find them. The heated breeze coming off the desert plains called to me. Whispered my name and pulled me in by an invisible tether. I couldn't explain it, but I knew I was meant to go there.

A smile crossed my lips. I was going.

# Two

## Scottie

The dying light had me pausing to look at my watch. Ma and Nan would have tea ready soon, and they expected us there and cleaned up when one of them rang the old cowbell hanging near the door. The air was cooling fast and being late autumn in the desert, darkness would be upon us quickly. The sky was already turning shades of purples and darker blues. This was my favourite time of year. The sun shined, but its heat wasn't as intense. Life was always slow-paced out here and after this muster, winter would come and we'd be able to relax a bit more. We had plenty to do—we always did—but the sun wasn't oppressive. It was a sight better working then than in summer.

The main homestead stood less than a hundred metres away, and even though I was a grown man, I wouldn't risk Nan's wrath by being late. I checked over the final coat of paint I'd just finished applying to the guesthouse. It was the original homestead, but it'd been a decade since anyone had lived in it. It'd lain vacant for years until we fixed it up, and for the last five years, we'd rented it out. Writers, artists, the odd family wanting their kids to have an outback experience, as well as a few scientists, had stayed out here of late.

The traditional Queenslander was modest. It was on stilts, raised a couple of feet off the ground, and had a wide staircase running up to the wrap-around veranda. Like all homesteads in the outback, it'd been handed down through the generations. Nan had moved in there with Pop when they'd been married sixty-six years ago. Pops had grown up on Pearce Station, and Nan was the girl next door—a four-hour car-ride away. He and Nan met as kids and fell in love. They went on to raise their girls in that house. As a kid, Ma had slept in a bedroom with her two sisters, their parents in the other one. There were only three other rooms in that house—a kitchen with a little table, a living room, and a bathroom that didn't have a dunny. There was an outhouse instead. I'd heard more than one story of snakes curled up in the corner, staying out of the winter cold. There was a shovel that hung from the dunny door which they used as a snake deterrent—as long as you didn't miss, you'd be right. Ma barely even blinked at snakes nowadays and even in her sixties was still as quick as a whip when beheading them. She had a healthy respect for them, but she wasn't scared. It was a trait she'd inherited from Nan and passed onto my sister. All the women that station produced were tough as nails and none took any shit.

While my aunts had grown up, left the station and now lived in the city, Ma had stayed on and proven to the old-timers that she deserved the title of stockman just as much as any of them. She ran the station side by side with Pops for years. On a trip to Sydney for the Royal Easter Show, she met my dad and they got hitched soon after. He followed her back to Pearce Station, but he was soon unhappy. I was sure he would have left sooner if he wasn't terrified of Pops. I understood how much of an adjustment it must have necessitated on his part moving from Sydney to the outback, but I couldn't fathom his desire to turn tail and leave. The red dirt was as much a part of me as my beating heart. It was in my soul. Ma shared the same love for the land. This desolate, unforgiving land was home. Rugged and brutal, I still marvelled at her beauty. The peace. The big skies and wide-open plains. The wildlife and even wilder locals. Everything about her called me to her and tethered me to this place. Not that I'd be anywhere else in the world, even if I could. This was where I belonged. But my dad, not so much. He pissed off when I was two days off turning thirteen and I hadn't seen him since.

I pushed thoughts of him aside. I had a lot to do before our guest arrived in the morning. The big-ticket item—the painting—was done. Now she was weather-proof again and ready for the upcoming summer. Ma and Nan looked after making sure the bed was made, and there were clean towels in there somewhere, and my sister, Ally, my five station hands, and I looked after the repairs to the fence in the smaller northern paddock. Age, the sun, and the animals meant that we were always repairing fences. The others were already out there and had been for a couple of days now. I was joining them tomorrow to wrap things up and bring back the supplies. They only had the ute with them and a few quad bikes. I had the Landcruiser at the homestead, so would make the hour-long trip out there in the morning, and we'd all be back for tea that night.

We were a working station—one I'd fought to sustain through the last few drought-ravaged years. Running cattle was my life, but the holiday accommodation was an important side earner for us. A four-hour drive away from Longreach airport, we were at an advantage over our neighbours out past the national parks to the west of the station and those to the south of us. So far, we'd been able to use it to keep us going during the hard times, even though we used a helluva lot more water with a guest.

I had a loyal crew. Thinking of them made me smile. I let it play on my lips, knowing that even though they wouldn't admit it, they'd love the idea of me calling them my family. Some were family by blood, some by choice. A rag-tag bunch, but family nevertheless. They all relied on me to make sure Pearce Station—our home—would be running for decades more to come. It was a responsibility I wore with pride. I walked back over to the main house. "Looks good, Scottie," Nan encouraged as I caught the screen door, stopping it from slamming.

"Too right." I grinned at her and dropped my hat on the hook by the door. Turning, I watched as the sun faded, marvelling at the beauty of the rainbow of colours in the sky. Running my fingers through my too-long hair, we stood at the window and watched as it dipped down over the horizon. The brilliant white of the old Queenslander stood in stark contrast to the red dirt and the purple-blue hues of the darkening sky. I loved the old place, and seeing Nan's eyes light up every time she saw how much the homestead again resembled the home she'd spent the happiest decades of her life in, rather than the going-on dilapidated and tired state it was in when Pops died, was reward enough.

I headed into the bathroom off my bedroom and washed with a sponge and a bucket-full of water, scrubbing my hair with shampoo and pursing my lips at the hints of grey at my temples, before dumping the water over my head to rinse it. None of us showered anymore. The water was too precious. We had to buy it from the city's water supply to fill up our tanks, so we never wasted it. The bores into the aquifer meant we had enough drinking water for the cattle, but even though it seemed endless, it wasn't. The water in the Great Artesian Basin was over two million years old and recharging what we used would take thousands of years. We never wasted a gift that the earth bestowed upon us. Especially when we knew how precious water was out here. The drought had wiped out any surface-level water supply years ago. The creek beds that only flowed during the wet season rains had been bone dry for seven years. Seven long years of dry wet seasons and even drier dry seasons. It'd been so long since we'd had decent rain that I wasn't even sure I remembered the sound of the drops on our old tin roof. I missed the noises and smells of the desert during the wet. Cicadas at night and frogs croaking down by the ponds and creeks and the whooshing of water flowing, bringing with it green grass and fields of wildflowers. The desert was so quiet now. As if it had gone to sleep waiting for the rains.

Even though we were remote, we weren't alone. Our neighbours—every station out west—were in the same predicament. The bores kept the cattle watered, but we hadn't been able to grow feed in years. Trucking it in was damned expensive—over ten grand a semi, and there was a wait list a mile long. But we had no other option. The only vegetation left in the ground was tinder dry—more of a fire hazard than food—and the land was parched. Buying feed pellets and bales of hay for the cattle to eat and getting it delivered was bleeding us dry. Two thousand head meant a lot of feed. But we'd survive. We always did.

The most important thing we had was hope. Conditions would improve. They always did. Eventually. The drought would break, and we'd increase our mob again. We could go back to growing our own feed and become self-reliant like we always were. All we had to do was hold out until then. And we would. I'd make sure of it. Ma always said I was as stubborn as her. I didn't see it like that. I preferred determined. This land was part of me, and I a part of it. I respected its power and our insignificance. We were lucky. Still operating on a three-year cycle, the money we spent today we had earned years earlier. Some were living year to year. Some month to month and drowning in debt.

With my thoughts preoccupied, I breathed in the delicious aroma of the roast chicken and veggies Ma had cooked for dinner. Warmth surrounded me, the heat from the big stove in the kitchen warming the room until it was toasty. In summer, we'd sit under the open windows, the cool evening breeze wafting over us, but the cold had settled in for the night. After helping to carry the tray over to the table, I sat and sighed, closing my eyes, always grateful for the land and our station. Contentment flowed over me. No matter what happened, the people around me, and this land, was home. It was peace and comfort. Friendship. And I loved it.

The table and benches in the large room were hand-fashioned from a monster of a blue gum tree. It'd been felled before there were controls on those kinds of things. Long and narrow, it ran the full length of the back of the house. The table had so many seats empty that night. It made me miss sleeping under the stars with my station hands. I didn't realize I'd voiced the thought until Ma nodded, adding, "I do too. But my old bones won't like it much if I tried it now."

Jono, my lead stockman and more of a father figure to me than my own dad had ever been, added, "Gets rough on us old folk."

I smiled. "My bones don't like it much either. But I still love it."

"I remember back before I'd had the girls when your pops and I used to muster together," Nan recalled with a wistful gleam in her eye. "The night sky was never-endin'. I'd lie there lookin' at it, mesmerized, for hours. The men would hit the hay and snore their heads off. But I'd be too busy lookin' up at the most incredible light show I've ever seen to fall asleep quickly."

I lifted my glass of water. "Here's to sleeping in the rough."

"Cheers," Nan added, clinking her cup of tea with my glass before bringing it to her lips.

"Thanks, Ma. This smells great." I breathed in deep again, enjoying the food I was loading onto my plate. We were quiet for a time while we ate, but my mind soon turned to the visitor beginning his stay the next day. He'd booked three months in the guesthouse, the longest stay we'd had yet. He'd be there right up until the wet season started, not that the long-range forecasts indicated any break in the drought. I hoped he was easy to get along with. We'd be sharing three meals a day with him, yet all I knew was his name—Peter McKenzie.

My destination was the closest fence in the smaller paddock immediately north of the homestead. We used it as a holding paddock of sorts, letting the calving cows give birth in there. It was a smaller area to keep an eye on when we needed the mob to be kept close. But like with any paddock, we had to upkeep the perimeter. That meant fencing.

I had the Landcruiser loaded with water and a fresh cooked breakfast for my stockmen well before dawn. I was driving, Jono in the passenger seat next to me. We took it easy travelling down the bumpy thirty-four K track because roos tended to jump towards the lights cast by the headlights, as did the damn stubborn echidnas. Hitting either one would screw up my plans for the day and probably put the Landcruiser out of action.

The sun rising to the east over the flat plains sent hues of pinks and gold shimmering across the sky. "I love this time of day," I sighed, Jono humming his agreement. The air still had the bite of oncoming winter chill to it, and the day held so much promise. As the sky turned to blue—the kind of rich, deep, crystal-clear blue I was sure was unique to the outback—I spotted the smoke from the campfire on the horizon. It curled into the cloudless sky wisp-like.

"No doubt Den's got a billy boiling. They'll be hungry," Jono mused.

"Good thing Ma stocked us up." I chuckled. There would be anarchy if their promised breakfast failed to materialize. The swags would have already been rolled, and they'd be cursing my name if I took too much longer to get there. The lure of two nights of drinking at the pub in Longreach was more than enough motivation to get stuck into the day's work and finish the fencing early.

We worked until the sun was high in the sky, replacing posts and wire fencing aged by the harsh desert conditions. It was brutal work, but bearable in the autumn sun rather than the inferno that it was during the summer months. There was always work to be done, but fencing was particularly hard during summer. Given how hard the muster was on the cattle, especially in such dry conditions, we moved the mob at a much slower pace. The muster had turned into a week-long trip under the blazing sun on horseback, motorbike, or in the utes on bumpy, dusty ground, with Jono in the chopper rounding up the rogues. But sleeping under the stars made up for that. Like Nan, I'd never get sick of admiring the view from down there on the red dirt. It was hard to beat a trillion stars twinkling overhead from one end of the horizon to the other. I was always at peace out there. The bellowing of the cattle as the mob lulled itself to sleep, and the crackle of the fire were two of my favourite sounds. But after hours of labour, it was hearing that final snip of the cutters on the fencing wire we'd just strung. I was helping Ally, Sam, Craig, and Den with this longer portion, while Jono, Waru, and Yindi had driven ahead to repair the last and smaller gap in the fence. Finished for the day, we loaded up the Landcruiser and headed their way in a convoy of quadbikes, with the four-wheel drive bringing up the rear. The bikes seemed to fly over the bumps and dips in the dirt track. I loved riding them. The Landcruiser had better suspension, making the ride easier for Jono, whose old bones couldn't handle a few hours on the bikes anymore. But the big car still bounced and shuddered when driving over the corrugations in the trail. It wasn't going to be a smooth ride for him. In less than a week, we'd be bringing the cattle down from the western paddock into the smaller holding yards. There, they'd be treated, tagged, and the bulls separated into another paddock. Those being sold would be loaded onto the trucks.

Less than two hours later, we were on the road home. Red dust plumed behind the quads, thickening the air and making it hard to breathe. I followed the others on a bike, and Jono brought up the rear of our convoy back to the homestead. Even though she was slower, I wished I was on horseback. My buckskin was a typical stock horse—a good fifteen hands and bred for endurance—but she was also my closest friend out here. It sounded ridiculous, but it was true. The aloneness, the peace got to me sometimes, and I held onto secrets I couldn't share. But Tilly didn't insist on words. All she needed was the wide-open plains and me, and she'd take me away so I could clear my head. It didn't take much to do it either. A few hours sitting in the shade of the big old eucalypt and I was usually feeling more like myself. I used to climb it when I was a kid—broke a couple of bones falling out of it too—but nowadays, it was just good to sit out in the shade and watch the eagles soar.

The collection of buildings near the homestead came into view on the horizon. The two sheds first. The bigger one housed our machinery—the big and small tractors, the chopper, the ute, Landcruiser, and the quads—and all the other stuff that needed storing. The smaller one was a stable for the horses. The dog kennel and chicken coop were to the back of that building and the three workers' cottages sat nearby. The original homestead—the one I'd painted the day before—was close too, with only the main homestead sitting separately. That was my father's doing. He'd wanted some space between he and Ma, Nan and Pops and the hands, but from the moment the house was built, everyone gathered there. I think that pissed him off the most.

I spied the Triton ute parked at the main homestead and wondered what our guest would be like. Our guests didn't usually stay as long as this bloke would be here for. The familiarity of everyone on the ranch made us a family. Living and working with them was everything. I hoped he fit in. Or at least wasn't obnoxious.

I wished he'd be someone I could connect with. Have something more than a friendship with, but I'd long ago given up that dream. It was impossible, and I was too old to believe that my Prince Charming would ride along on his white horse anyway. I wasn't out and I never would be. My sister always complained that there were no eligible bachelors around, but at least she had options. I had the choice of bugger all and none. Everyone knew Scottie Pearce, owner of Pearce Station. I had a station to run and it wouldn't go down well to be known as a limp-wristed poofter. I'd be lucky if I wasn't laughed out of town and even luckier if I managed to avoid a black eye and a few broken ribs each and every time I ventured off the station. Oh, and there was the minor issue of every one of my suppliers and contractors likely refusing to do business with us anymore. I'd headed up Pearce Station for nearly twenty years—half my life, but that wouldn't count for anything. It was no secret that the old-timers still thought women couldn't manage stations because they weren't strong enough. Ma had showed most of them, and Ally was doing a bloody good job of keeping them in their place, but they also regarded both as more of a bloke than a sheila anyway. But a gay man? There'd be no hope he'd be accepted—no hope I'd be accepted. I loved my pops but hearing the diatribe when for a few hours once a year SBS played footage of Mardi Gras on the tele was never easy. Knowing I'd disgust him if he knew the truth about me was the worst part. I'd idolized him growing up. Wanted to be just like him. Professionally, I was just like him. I'd managed the station successfully and even though conditions were the toughest we'd seen in generations, I was doing a damn good job of it. But I knew I could never truly be myself.

So, despite my burning curiosity about what our visitor would be like, I unloaded the vehicles and refuelled them before dusting the red dirt off my clothes and climbing the veranda steps. It was hard to keep the fine dust out of the house, and Ma always knew before I'd even stepped two feet inside if I'd failed to brush myself off. Toeing my boots off, I carried them in. Visitors of the eight-legged variety were not the kind I liked to find hiding out in them. While my boots had a spot under the peg on which I hung my hat, there was a new set in the way. Decent quality, but brand new. Any hope I'd had of the visitor having spent time in the outback before fled. I'd be babysitting for months if he wanted to head out yonder because new boots and a new hat—with a bright shiny buckle of all things—meant one thing: inexperience. The desert was no place for wearing in new footwear. He was probably some hipster rich kid who was finding his zen in the outback. Either that or a middle-aged bloke going through a midlife crisis who wanted to prove to his late forty-something-year-old body that he could still have an adventure. Shame they'd miss the fancy coffee.

My first impression wasn't great, and while I knew I should at least meet the bloke, the excitement of seeing a new face dimmed. I ran my fingers through my hair, pushing it back off my forehead before walking through the door to the heart of our house, the kitchen. The floor creaked underfoot and all the eyes in the large room were suddenly on me. But I couldn't speak. All I could do was stare.

Tall, lean, and nothing like I'd pictured. Absolutely not a middle-aged wannabe.

He was a kid—nineteen at most. Baby-faced and gorgeous. Breathtaking in fact. Where my hair was brown and my skin tanned from countless hours outdoors, our guest's hair was a rich copper colour, which I just knew would glint gold in the sunlight. Freckles dotted his nose and cheeks, together with his pale forearms, which were currently resting on the table, a cuppa sitting nearby. His emerald green eyes caught and held my gaze, and skin as smooth as a baby's bottom framed plump, totally kissable lips that quirked up in a half smile when he saw me. He was completely unexpected and undoubtedly beautiful.

I was screwed. Totally fucked.

Ma spoke first. "Scottie, you lookin' to trap some flies?"

"Ma," I mumbled, flushing and looking down at the floor. I didn't wait for her to add anything else, instead forcing my legs to move. Holding my hand out to our guest, I introduced myself. "Scottie." He grasped my hand and shook with a firm grip. His palms were warm and smooth, but I expected that with a bloke who didn't look like he'd ever spent the day outdoors. "You must be Peter."

"Pete, please. Or Macca. Either way I don't mind." His voice was deep and rumbly, a contrast to his youthful appearance. Cultured, even though he used the shortened versions of both his first and last names. He went to withdraw his hand from my grasp, and like an idiot, I shook it again. I wanted to slap myself across the back of the head, but instead, I withdrew my hand and shoved it in my pocket to stop fidgeting.

"You, ah, far from home, Pete?"

"A little." He smiled and my dick twitched in my pants. I froze, then panicked and dropped onto the closest bench, hoping he hadn't gotten an eyeful of the thickening bulge in my jeans. I clenched my jaw tight and nodded my encouragement for him to keep speaking. I didn't trust my voice not to crack like a teenager's. "I'm from Sydney, so yeah, a little ways away."

Ally stuck her head through the door, her hair still wet from washing it. Dressed in fresh jeans and a tee, she looked cute and her smile at our new visitor was coy. "Hey, new guy," she greeted, smiling at him.

My gaze cut to Peter's again, and he looked her up and down, smiling. This time, my dick didn't twitch. My temper did. My sister was no wallflower—she could handle everything on the station as well as any one of us could—but I'd be damned if I stood by while this city boy flirted with her.

"Scottie here has no manners, and Nan and Ma will keep you chatting all day. Want me to show you round before tea?"

He looked at me for a beat too long before turning away and smiling at her, smug grin and all. I scowled. I hated him already. "Sure."

He pushed up from the table, and even though I was pissed with him, I was glad I was sitting down. He wore a faded grey T-shirt that draped itself loosely over his shoulders and arms that I wanted to feel wrapped round me. Hooked under my shoulders or wrapped round them. Either way would work. He pushed himself up and the pale skin on his arms caught my attention again. The smattering of red hair and freckles just made his fair tone stand out more. It was such a contrast to my darker tan and the others out here that my mouth watered. I trailed my gaze slowly up to his throat and wondered if the freckles I saw there extended down to his chest.

Every dirty fantasy exploded in my mind, and I had to bite back a groan as he stepped over the bench he was sitting on and I got a look at his lower half. Well-worn blue jeans that hugged every inch of his long legs greeted me. Legs that left me in no doubt he was fit. He reached for my sister's outstretched hand.

"I'm Ally," she said, shaking it. It wasn't the no-nonsense, bone-crushing shake that she normally reserved for everyone. It was giggly and she blushed. Then she went and fluttered her eyes at him. Who was this girl and what had she done with my sister, the kick-arse stockman? And yes, stockman, not stockwoman. That was something she'd clip you for—calling her something different than all of us.

My blood boiled, white-hot jealousy flaring in me. My reaction was completely uncalled for. I knew that. But it didn't mean I had to like it. I shouldn't get jealous of my sister. She deserved to be happy, and she had a better bloody chance of it than I ever did. Shame filled me, an unwanted emotion that I tried to push away, but instead, my gut dropped to the floor. Disappointment flooded in, even though I shouldn't have even let myself hope for a millisecond that it would be any other way. That it could be any other way than me being alone. I'd spent so much time persuading myself that I didn't need any of that relationship stuff—the hand-holding and kissing, the quiet moments just the two of us, the living and working together, the sex— that I'd ignored the truth. I wanted it all. Especially the sex. I really wanted that. It'd only taken this stranger a moment in time to turn that on its head. He was going to wreak havoc on my ordered, simple life. Then he'd leave. Or he'd sleep with my sister. Either way, I just knew the next three months couldn't end soon enough.

# THREE

## Pete

"So, you ridden before?" Ally asked me as we walked. She was about ten years older than me, but she didn't act like it. I could already tell she was a bit of an adrenaline junkie. We'd toured all the buildings and I'd dropped my bag into the guest quarters that was a way away from the main house. The paddock we were now entering was on the other side of the guesthouse. We headed towards the corrugated iron shed, which looked like an empty barn, but we didn't go in there. Instead, Ally opened a gate that abutted the building, and we passed the feed and water troughs lining the wall in the shade. Before us was a paddock, five or six acres at a guess, and I could see horses—the most beautiful animals I'd ever seen—walking among the brush. Ally let out a short, sharp whistle and the largest animal, a dark brown one with a large white patch on its side cantered over. My heart pounded in my chest as I watched the horse get closer and closer without stopping, only to come up short a few feet from Ally. Shaking its mane and stamping its foot, the horse huffed and nudged her, pushing her back a step.

"Hey, girl," she soothed. I barked out a laugh when the mare, who also had a white diamond on her nose, nudged

Ally again. "Yeah, yeah," she muttered, holding out an apple to the horse. "I know I haven't been here in a coupla days and we haven't been riding in ages, but I bought a peace offering. Here." She held it out to the horse, and once she'd taken it, Ally turned back to me. "This is 'Tella, short for Nutella."

"She's beautiful. Big too. The others aren't as big as she is, are they?" I hesitated to get closer, and Ally side-eyed me.

"You aren't confident with 'em, are you?" she stated rather than asked, her distaste obvious in her pursed lips.

"I've ridden before, but it was a long time ago. I just didn't want to overstep boundaries. What are the rules about petting a lady's horse?"

Without an ounce of hesitation, she whipped back, "It's not the same as petting a lady, so feel free to give her a rub." I froze and looked at the firecracker standing before me. She raised her eyebrow at me, and I choked out an embarrassed laugh. Jesus. She was forthright; I liked her already.

"Ah." I hesitated, not even knowing how to respond. If I was at home, I would have snapped a retort back about knowing how to handle men rather than women, but I didn't fancy outing myself among a bunch of strangers. I needed them. I needed to be allowed to stay. Ally rolled her eyes and laughed at me before motioning for me to pet Nutella. The horse's hair was coarser than I remembered, and the strength I could feel in her muscles was awe-inspiring. The ponies I'd ridden as a kid were so different to these fully grown workhorses. I cast my gaze around the paddock, and my eyes locked on the sight before me. The head of Pearce Station was having a quiet moment with a horse I guessed was his. Brushing down its neck and standing real close to the powerful animal. It was almost intimate.

He was nothing like I imagined. Scott Pearce was older—probably late thirties, with grey around his temples. But damn… model-worthy. Not one of those catalogue perfect men who looked like it took hours to style their artfully messy do, but real and strong and mussed up and covered in red dirt and sexy as hell. A few centimetres shorter than me, but with a strength that I could tell was from endless hours of hard work rather than sculpted in a gym. Broad shoulders, a narrow waist, long legs, and from what I could see, an arse I could bounce a coin off. When he'd clasped my hand with his work-roughened one, I was hard-pressed not to moan out loud. His grip was firm. Controlled. I bet he could have crushed my hand if he tried, but he didn't. In fact, he seemed to hesitate. He moved with this relaxed swagger, like everything operated on his say so, and I supposed it did. It was clear that the women on the station—Karen and Lynn—were the matriarchs of the family and held as much, if not more, sway than he did, but Scott had presence. I was only with him for a matter of a minute, but I hadn't been able to get him out of my head since. And now, seeing him in what seemed like a private moment with his horse, I was even more drawn to him.

"Scottie's horse is Tilly," Ally said from behind me, jogging to catch up. I hadn't realized I'd walked away from her towards him. "She's a buckskin." The golden horse stood smaller than Nutella. Her dark mane shone as Scott brushed her down. Calmer than Ally's mount, she stood patiently as Scott moved to her legs. The two of them silhouetted by the setting sun made for a stunning vista. Endless kilometres of flat red earth dotted with blue-green vegetation stretched out, and the range in the far distance was quickly turning shades of purple. The darkening blue of the sky was tinged with the remainders of pinks and oranges as the sun sank into the horizon for the day. Lost for words, I stared. The view—the whole view—was spectacular. "Wow," I breathed, coming up beside Scott and reaching for Tilly, petting her neck. The big horse turned to me, nudging me in the shoulder as I kept petting her.

"She likes you," Scott said quietly, wonder in his voice. "She's usually a bit of a loner."

"You're a beautiful girl, aren't ya?" I cooed to her, immediately more comfortable in her presence than 'Tella's. Scott's lips tilted up in a small smile. He wasn't looking at me. His gaze was focussed on his horse as he absently brushed down her mane again, but I was watching him. The serious expression he wore in the kitchen was gone, the frown line on his forehead smooth, and the set of his shoulders relaxed. He turned to me and our eyes met and held. It might have been only a second, or an entire week, but I wanted nothing more for it to have been a moment between us. My breath caught and my heart pounded in my chest, my pulse thrumming hard through my veins as I thought about being able to reach out and touch him.

About what he'd taste like and how his rough hands would feel on my bare skin. I didn't realize I'd moved closer until Scott sidestepped, moving around me. Embarrassment and more than a little regret washed over me. There I was, imagining the perfect moment, a first kiss to ruin me for all other men, and a sweaty roll around in the sack with a sexy-as-hell farmer who was probably straighter than an arrow. But what was the likelihood that I'd find a gay farmer five hundred Ks past the middle of nowhere? None and Buckleys, that's what.

The hot flush to my skin must have given me away. Being a ranga meant that my pale complexion turned beet red every time I did something stupid, like imagine the sexy stockman underneath me as I rode him.

"You, ah... wanna go for a ride sometime?" Scott asked. The question seemed to surprise him, if his wide-eyed stare was anything to go by. Or maybe it was just the way he worded his invitation. "I mean—"

"I'd love to." I smiled at him and nodded. "See a bit more of the place, that is." I waved my hand out towards the ranges and the spot where the sun had just sunk below the horizon. All the maps, all the hours of searching... the singular focus on my goal. The rush to get out here. But now I was there, my world had tilted on its axis. It suddenly didn't seem as important to find the reef. Other priorities occupied my mind. "You know, help out a bit." I didn't know what I was saying. I was adequate enough with dirt. Okay, at identifying soil properties and rock types. I was better with history. With books and with the ghosts of yesteryear.

I was what you'd typically call a nerd—reading glasses and all. I'd ridden horses before, but I wasn't an expert by any means, and I had no idea what the hell to do with a cow. Never mind a herd of them. But at that moment, none of it mattered. I wanted to get to know how this station worked. I wanted to be out on the land, to feel a part of something bigger—the red dirt and blue skies. Inexplicably, this piece of Australia felt important to me, and I couldn't ignore the pull it had over me.

Ally stood beside me and smiled. I'd forgotten she was there. I tried to smile at her, but truthfully, I was kind of annoyed by her interruption. Bound to happen though. We couldn't exactly stand out here all night, and even if I did, why would Scott want to? It wasn't like he was going to get all romantic and hold my hand while we strolled back through the darkened paddocks to the guesthouse. I gave her a small smile but spun back to Scott when he knocked his shoulder into mine as he walked past. Before I could call him out on his shit, Ally spoke. "Dinner's up. Freshen up and come straight back to the house. I'll see you in there."

The hot water of the shower felt great on my skin after the two-thousand-kilometre drive I'd made over the last few days. My body hurt, my muscles ached, and I was tired. But excitement filled me. The beauty of the outback had stolen my breath. The people—Scott—intrigued me too. Not that I could let myself be distracted by dreaming about a completely unavailable man. I'd made that cliched mistake before.

The warmth of the autumn day in the desert had faded with the lengthening shadows of dusk, and a chill had set in by the time I'd made it to the house and bounded up the steps to the back door. I was glad I'd worn my jacket, even for the short walk to the homestead. The table was set for five when I walked in and the others were already sitting down. No one had started eating yet, and Scott didn't look impressed at all with the delay.

"Ah, thanks for waiting? I guess I'm late."

"Tea is at six sharp every night," Karen, the grandmother, scolded. I gave her a sheepish smile and sat at the only remaining place setting, right next to Scott.

"Ally should have told you," her mother said, sending a dirty look Ally's way. Ally looked away, embarrassment tinting her cheeks.

"I offered to go get him." She shrugged.

From my peripheral vision, I saw Scott tense up and let out a low noise that sounded almost like a growl. He slowly put his cutlery down and blew out a breath. "Did she mention any of the other house rules while you two were getting cosy together on your walk?"

"Look, I...." I trailed off, not wanting to offend any of them. Ally was friendly, but not overly flirty. I didn't think she was hitting on me but buggered if I knew whether I was right or wrong. "We were talking horses and the muster you've got coming up."

Scott huffed and shook his head. "Station rules: One: we're a dry station. No alcohol past the front gates. You wanna drink, go to Longreach. We have six hands apart from Ally and me—that's where they are now. You'll meet them the day after tomorrow. If you wanna go to church, go with Nan, Ma, and Ally. They're leaving first thing and they'll be back late arvo. They go every month.  Two: brekkie is at half five, lunch at noon, and tea at six. Breakfast and lunch on Sundays are always make your own. Three: no hat, no shoes, and no dusty clothes inside. Four: keep your showers short—we're trucking in water so wasting it on showers is expensive—"

I put my hand up and Scott stopped mid-sentence. "Wait, you're trucking in water? You don't have a water source out here? I thought you'd have bores into the Basin."

"We draw water from the Artesian Basin for the cattle. We can't sustainably grow feed out here unless it rains, and we don't use bore water to fill up the tanks. It's not environmentally sustainable—the water in the Basin's thousands of years old. Some estimates make it a couple of million, so if we're drawing too much out of it, the water depletes. Not everyone has the same attitude, but we graze as sustainably as possible. That means we buy water for us and feed for the animals. We'll have a truck arrive while we're doing the muster so while they're all in the confined yard, we'll have some fresh feed for them."

"Fuck," I muttered, then winced as Karen glared at me. Country manners meant no swearing at the table. Or in front of the ladies really. They could probably curse up a storm better than I ever could, but I wanted to show my respect. I felt like I needed to. If I were being honest, I'd say that all three women were intimidating in their own way. I supposed they had to be strong out here. Where Scott had presence and commanded respect by the way he carried himself, the three women of Pearce Station put the fear of getting castrated in you. "Sorry, ma'am. I apologize."

She gave me an approving smile, and said, "Call me Nan. Everyone does."

Scott kept up the hard-arsed boss routine, and Ally rolled her eyes at everything he said. Except for one thing.

"Final rule and most important. Never go anywhere by yourself or without telling someone where you're going. Always take water and a sat phone, and during autumn and in winter, a foil blanket. No exceptions. The weather's right now, but you'll need the blanket at night. As it gets warmer—and it's gonna—you'll only survive for a couple of days without water. You get lost or hurt and we don't know where to find you... we'll be recovering a body."

Ally nodded, and I swallowed hard. Reality hit me like a Mack Truck. I'd planned on driving out to the reef and camping there for a few days at a time just to cover as much ground as I could without wasting fuel and daylight hours. I knew I'd have to buy diesel off the station, but I didn't know how much they had in reserve. I had to prospect without any real equipment—a metal detector a shovel, crowbar, and a plastic trowel were about the only tools I was permitted to use with the license I held, so prospecting for those few hours each day I'd otherwise spend travelling, was important. That was still the plan, I supposed. It might be nice to have some company though. I looked at Scott and mentally head-slapped myself. What was I thinking? I was asking for trouble even imagining him being there with me.

"So, Pete, what brings you here?" Lynn asked. I hesitated. I'd sent them a copy of the prospecting permit just like I was supposed to do to give notice of entry onto the property. My name was on both that application and the booking I'd made through Airbnb. Hadn't they pieced it together? I was out there for the reef. To find Byron's lost gold. But even only having been on the station for a few hours, I knew there was something more that I'd find there. It was a place like nowhere on earth I'd been, and I wanted to experience it for all its rugged glory. I wanted to get to know the people too. Find out what made them tick. Or a certain someone anyway.

Maybe that was why I didn't tell them the full truth. Maybe I was just being a coward. "I'm a historian and I have a degree in geology. I wanted to experience it myself, I suppose. See what the pioneers saw. Follow in their footsteps." I paused, realizing the truth of my words as I spoke them. "And I want to learn about farming here. The challenges, the highs and lows."

"We're a station, not a farm," Lynn corrected. "Farms are smaller than stations. We graze cattle, so we're graziers, not farmers—"

"It's a harsh life," Nan added, "But I wouldn't live anywhere else even if I could. Bloody perfect if you ask me."

"It's pretty special," I agreed, not daring to look up from my plate. I could feel the flush heating my cheeks.

Dinner had long finished, and Nan and Lynn—who'd insisted I call her Ma—had retired inside. Ally, Scott, and I sat on cut logs around a small fire toasting marshmallows. We weren't talking much. I was enjoying just being outside in the open space, the quiet of the night surrounding us. It was something so different from what I was used to. Apartment living in Sydney had its perks. I could go downstairs and within five minutes, I had the choice of pretty much any food I could dream up. There was a beauty to the city, especially the harbour. Sunlight glinting off the water, the boats and ships sailing under the bridge. The white peaks of the Opera House. I could sit in a café, drink fancy coffee and people-watch all day long if I wanted to. But at the same time, it was noisy and crowded. People were miserable, always running here or there. Never even looking up to see what was around them to enjoy the moment. Phones and smog and traffic. Crowded and cluttered and always busy. Always racing. Here, time seemed to slow. I could breathe easier. And the sky. Even with the light pollution from the fire and the nearby porch light, I could see that the sky was alight. Millions—probably billions—of tiny pinpricks of light twinkled above. Even the half-moon seemed bigger somehow. Closer.

I was watching the firelight playing on Scott's features when Ally spoke. "I need to hit the hay. Macca, want me to walk you to your room?"

I never broke my stare away from Scott, and there was no hesitation in my response either. "Nah, I'll find my way back. Night, Ally."

"Night," Scott said while pushing the logs in the fire around with a stick. He had his knees spread, his elbows resting on them as he leaned toward the fire. His hair had flopped forward, the satiny strands looking soft in the muted light. I wondered if they'd slide through my fingers like the touch of silk. I blinked, knowing I couldn't go down that path with him and turned my attention back to the flickering flames.

"If you wanna ask me something, just ask it," Scott spoke quietly after a time.

"Does it get lonely out here?" It wasn't what I wanted to ask, but it was as close as I dared come to the question I really wanted to know the answer to.

"Yes and no. We're only a few hours out of Longreach, so it's easy enough to go there. Everyone else usually does."

"But not you," I finished.

"Nah, I stay here and look after the animals when they all head off."

"You can't go to town on one of the weekends your station hands stay here?"

He shook his head. "Not really much point. I don't really drink." He shrugged. "And I don't do church either so...."

I sat quietly for a moment, contemplating what he said. "How old are you?"

"Forty. You?"

"Twenty-five." When he flicked his gaze to mine, shock lit his features. "I look younger, I know. It's the freckles." He nodded and I hedged another question. "You don't wanna hook up with anyone in town? Find a nice lady to spend the night with? This station's a long way from company. Don't you crave sex?"

He looked hard at me, unflinching. As if he was analysing what I was asking. Searching for a deeper meaning. I was, and yet I wasn't. Granted, he was a few years older than me, but he was still a man. He still had urges. Needs. He ran the station and had the respect of his family. I hadn't seen him with his stockmen and women, but I had a feeling they'd respect him all the same. And yet he lived in a bubble. Seemed to isolate himself.

"I go to the Royal Easter Show and the Ekka every year. It's enough."

"Fuck me, you're a better man than me. I'd go stir crazy."

"Yeah well, just shows how different we are."

There was a bite to his tone, which I hadn't meant to put there. "I didn't mean to offend you."

His voice was quiet, but there was steel behind it. That same charisma turned into passion and fire. "We don't all have the luxury of being able to walk into a bar somewhere and fuck the first person to catch your eye. Longreach is a small town. Everyone knows everyone. I can't just go round and hook-up with whoever I like. It'd have consequences. For my family. For this station. And I won't risk either one of them just to get my rocks off." His eyes flashed angrily and his nostrils flared as he breathed hard.

"I'm sorry, I didn't know."

He sighed. "Don't apologize. I just can't. Ma and Nan, even Ally are always at me to go out and meet some girl I can bring home. But that's not me. Longreach is in the middle of bloody nowhere, but we're even more remote. This desert... it's in me. It's part of my soul. I reckon if you cut me, I'd bleed red dirt. But it's a hard life. One that most people won't even consider." He poked at the fire again. With his head down and his shoulders sagging, he spoke again, his voice barely above a whisper, "It's easier not to try. No disappointment...." His words trailed off like he'd expended all the energy he had.

"You have your family and your workers. At least you're not alone." I snapped the twig I'd used to toast marshmallows on and tossed it into the dying embers of the fire that were being kept alive by Scott's prodding. "Apart from hook-ups, and a flatmate I saw every few days, I didn't really have anyone. And we all know how deep and meaningful hook-ups are."

"No parents? Siblings?"

"An older sister, but apparently I embarrass her, so I tend to just keep away. Mum and Dad don't understand. They mean well, but they keep trying to change me into something I'm not. And it's hard to make friends in the city when you don't get out much other than to get off."

"Tough gig, huh?" he mused. "Suppose you don't need to be in the desert to be isolated."

"That's the funny thing with a city. You can be alone and lonely even in the biggest crowd." I gave him a small smile, trying to shake off the downer I'd plunged us into. I stood up then and stretched my arms above my head before a yawn ripped free. "Come on, walk me to my room so I don't break a leg or stand on a snake. Get eaten by a dingo. Whatever."

"Dingoes don't usually bother us, especially not near the homestead. We don't bait them 'cause they naturally keep the roo population from exploding, but we've got to protect the calves from them. We run Charbray cattle here—a Charolais Brahman cross—so they're too big for the dingoes to attack when they're fully grown. But, yeah...."

"I'm smaller than a cow. Seriously, are they gonna eat me?" My alarm was clear.

Scott laughed and my breath caught in my throat. His entire face transformed. Years fell away and a smile worthy of a Hollywood actor spread across his features. "You'll be right, mate." He clapped me on the shoulder, and I swallowed. "Come on, City. Let's get you tucked into bed. We get up early here."

I ignored the jibe, still speechless from seeing his smile, and followed him into the darkness. It took a moment for my eyes to adjust, but when they did, I saw the silhouette of the guesthouse against the starry sky. The building wasn't what captured my attention though. It was the stars. An immense sky touched the horizon all around us. Bright pinpricks of light pierced the darkness and the half-moon hovering there seemed like I could reach out and touch it. The flat land extended for hundreds of kilometres in every direction. Dark and quiet, it was a complete contrast with the fireworks show in the sky. I didn't realize I'd stopped walking until Scott stepped up beside me, our shoulders nearly touching, and looked up too. "Nothing like the sky out here."

"It's beautiful," I breathed, looking at him with wonder in my eyes. When he turned to me, I couldn't help adding, "But everything out here is."

"Ally'll be pleased to hear that," he huffed and turned away, stomping up the steps of the guesthouse and opening the door. He held it open for me, waiting until I'd walked past him before turning on his heel and striding away. His mood swings could give anyone whiplash, but what he'd confided in me made me think that, perhaps, it wasn't a nice girl he wanted to bring home. Or maybe it was just blind hope.

"Scott?" I called.

"Scottie. Not Scott. What?"

"I wasn't talking about Ally." I paused for a moment and added, "Night," before closing the door. I didn't wait for a response. I knew I wouldn't get one. I just hoped he didn't come back and beat me to a pulp for making a comment like that. Hoped that the next morning I still had a place at their table.

# FOUR

## Scottie

I stopped walking as soon as his words registered. "I wasn't talking about Ally." Was he speaking about me? I'd felt his eyes on me by the campfire. I thought I'd been imagining it. I thought it'd been wishful thinking on my part. A goofy smile tilted my lips upward instead of the frown I'd had only a moment ago. My mood swings had been off the charts since I'd seen him. I was grateful no one had called me out on them. I was surprised Ally hadn't. She and Nan had a knack for giving me a kick up the arse, making me pull my head out.

I kicked the sandy dirt over the dying embers of the fire before bounding up the steps to the homestead. I closed up, turned out the lights—except the one on the veranda in case Pete needed it—and stripped my clothes off on the way to my bedroom. I dumped all of them in the hamper and fell into bed with just my undies on. I didn't even have the energy to brush my teeth, even though my body was kind of buzzing.

The smile didn't leave my lips as I fell asleep, and I was still wearing it the next morning when I woke up with the sun. We'd stayed up late the night before. Well after every-one else had gone to bed. I'd only had a few hours of shut-eye, but it was enough. I had a spring in my step as I pulled on a pair of jeans, a faded tee, and a red and white check flannie. The house was still quiet when I went outside to do my morning rounds. Fresh hay for the horses, meat for the dogs, and pellets and kitchen scraps for the chickens. Water for all of them as well as giving a sprinklin' to Nan's veggie patch. I let the dogs out into the covered yard and the horses into the paddock they spent their days in before mucking out their stalls and the dogs' kennels and meandering back to the homestead.

"Hey, Scottie," Pete called out from behind me. I turned and grinned at him. He was wearing jeans and a T-shirt, a pretty light one for so early in the morning, but he looked good. Those brand-new boots were on his feet and he jogged over to me. When he got close, he scrunched up his nose all cute like and frowned. "What the hell is that smell?"

"Horse shit most likely." I shrugged. "Mucked out the stables after I fed the animals."

"Oh, okay. Sorry. I, ah, didn't mean to offend."

"You say that a lot, you know?" I looked at him and raised my eyebrow. "Sorry. You've got nothing to be sorry for. Takes a bit more to upset me than someone telling me I stink."

"Force of habit. Bump into someone you say sorry, you want to talk to someone you say sorry for the interruption. Just the way it seems to go at home."

"Well, you don't have to be sorry for anything out here unless you swear at the table or kill Nan's veggie patch.

Then I'd run. If you hear them full-naming ya, you're already too late."

Pete smirked at me and I grinned back, both turning into a laugh when we both added, "But you gotta come back sometime, boy."

"My mum used to say that to me all the time when I was a kid. I'd do something—usually eat the biscuits she'd baked for visitors, or something stupid like that—and I'd get busted. I was already out the door by that stage. My best mate lived a few doors down, so I'd sprint over to his place and Mum would call out 'you gotta come back sometime, Peter Jackson McKenzie.'"

"I'd get into the scones, then jump the fence into the horses' paddock, mount my horse bareback, and tear off through the scrub. Ma would yell it too." I held the door open for him, and he peered in the bucket I was carrying. I'd collected the eggs from the chickens that morning too.

"Organic free range?" he quipped as he strode past me, stopping at the kitchen bench.

I spoke in my best telemarketing voice. I sounded like Ray Martin, a journalist from the city. He was famous Australia-wide. "Here at Pearce Station, we strive to provide the highest level of service and quality using the best, organic produce on the market, grown and harvested locally. Now get off your arse and help me cook breakfast. You're on tea duty."

"Tell me you have a coffee machine," he begged.

"Ah, no?" I hedged. "We might have some instant somewhere in the pantry. We all drink Bushells."

"Tea?" He half groaned, half sobbed, the sound full of pain. I couldn't help my laugh as I ducked into the nearby bathroom and cleaned myself up, ready to start cooking. When I walked back in, Pete was standing in front of the stove, two mugs on the bench, one with a tea bag in it while he was stabbing the dried-up coffee in the tin of Nescafé he'd obviously found somewhere in the pantry. I started frying up some bacon and cracked the eggs to scramble them while watching him with a smirk.

"Buck up, City. I'll ask Ma to swing by the supermarket if it's open. You'll have your fancy coffee tomorrow."

"Fancy coffee has a pattern sprinkled onto the foam and a shot of something in it." He looked at me pleadingly and added, "But yeah, if your mum could get me something drinkable, I'd appreciate it. Otherwise, I might not be fun to live with over the next couple of days while I detox."

"You drink that much?" I asked, surprised, just as Ally walked through the door. She was dressed for church, wearing a knitted white jumper and a pair of dark blue jeans with clean boots. Her Akubra was missing off her head, her straight brown hair shiny instead of in a ponytail like she normally kept it.

Her smile turned into a scowl, and she spoke louder than necessary in an almost shout. "You're coming here to get sober? You're an alcoholic and, what, you thought it'd be right to come here while you're detoxing? We're hours away from the doc. You can't stay here."

"Relax, Ally. He was talking about coffee, not liquor. Telling me he likes it with fancy patterns and shots of flavour.

He's probably one of those people who never makes it himself. Buys every cup from coffee artisans."

"Not always. I had a coffee machine at home," he defended. But even I could tell it was half-hearted. I could easily see him being one of those coffee snobs.

"Good to know." Ally huffed and snatched a piece of bacon that I'd placed on a plate.

"What's all the hullabaloo?" Nan asked as she walked in, travel mug already in hand.

"Nothin', Nan." I smiled and kissed her on the cheek. She always made the effort to dress up for church on the Sundays they went, and today was no exception. She looked dainty in her dress and hat. Through the kitchen window, I could see Ma walking towards the shed that housed the Landcruiser. She was dressed much the same.

I always looked forward to Sunday mornings. Me, my horse, and a few hours of quiet. It was my time. My chance to ride out to wherever I wanted and sit and enjoy the changing landscapes. The creek was long dry, but when it used to flow, I'd ride to it and take a dip. Nowadays I go there just to sit and watch the colours morph in the changing sun. There was a seam of white quartz interlaced through the gully that glinted in the sunlight as if it was filled with diamonds. They weren't, but it didn't matter. I still loved it there. My tree—the big old eucalypt—sat on the high side of the ridge overlooking the land for kilometres. It was where I wanted to go, where I usually needed to go to clear my head. My conversation last night with our visitor had rattled me. He'd asked some questions that I came awfully close to answering.

It wasn't the questions that had bothered me. I wasn't lying when I told Pete that I wasn't easily offended, and he needed to stop apologizing. No, it was my reaction to them. I'd had so much practice redirecting conversations that I was an expert at it. At changing subjects and giving non-answers to probing questions. I didn't want to lie to my family but telling them the truth was impossible too, so I deflected. Out here, when one person knew, it was as good as telling everyone. The gossip vine was alive and kicking. We were out in the desert, in some of the most sparsely populated land in Australia, but it didn't matter. People in town would find out before I'd even managed to get off the property, and that'd be the end of anyone dealing with Pearce Station.

But when Pete asked me whether I craved sex, and the conversation led down the path it had, I'd had to bite my tongue to stop myself from telling him that disappointment was a real risk for me. If I didn't try, I'd never confirm I was the only gay man for hundreds of Ks. Even if there were others, it was even less likely that one would take my fancy. I'd discovered yesterday afternoon that my tastes lent more towards a young Prince Harry lookalike than the typical deeply suntanned fella out here.

I dished up mine and Pete's breakfast, and we sat as Ma brought round the Landcruiser and Ally followed Nan out to the car. Within moments, the only sounds were the scraping of cutlery on the china plates and a quiet moan as Pete leaned back and patted his flat belly. "There's only one thing that would make that breakfast perfect." He sighed.

"Coffee?"

"Coffee."

I laughed at his predictability, but I felt his pain. I'd hate to imagine the fallout if we ran out of tea at the station. We'd have a mutiny. So him not having coffee would suck just as much.

"I asked Ma before they left. She'll get the good stuff for you."

"I could kiss you right now," Pete blurted, then turned to me wide-eyed and stammered, "Ah, you know... ah...."

Was it stupid that my heart stuttered in my chest? That it beat a little harder and a shot of what felt a lot like adrenaline whizzed through my veins? He didn't know about me—at least I didn't think he did. *Is gaydar a real thing?* If it was, I didn't have it. Could he be gay? Maybe that was why we seemed to get along so well, despite my being nearly old enough to be his father. We had that little, but fundamental, piece of ourselves in common. Could I be projecting much? It was impossible. Well, not *impossible* impossible, but on a scale of one to ten of likely, it had to be about minus five. Surely. There was no way. It was just a saying. Had to be.

"Figure of speech, I get it. Relax."

His shoulders dropped and he let out a breath. His whole reaction would have been almost comical, if I didn't recognize his absolute fear. But was it fear of being mistaken for gay or a fear of being discovered? At opposite ends of the spectrum, I hoped it was the latter. If it was the former, it was going to be an even longer three months than I'd thought.

"So, what did you have planned today?" Pete asked me as he picked up his fork and speared a piece of scrambled egg. "I don't want to get in your way, but I can help if you have stuff you need to do."

"Stuff?" I asked, one eyebrow raised. "Real particular there, huh?"

"I dunno what really happens on a farm—sorry, station—so yeah, stuff."

He shrugged, and the uncertainty reflected off him. On anyone else—my city-boy father for example—it would have been annoying as hell, but on him, it was endearing. I sobered at that. We all knew what happened with city folk around here. They left. Pete might have been sticking round for a few months but come spring and he'd be out of here. Back to air-con. Back to swimming at the beach. Back to nightclubs and whatever else he liked to get up to. As much as I'd discovered the night before that I liked him, I couldn't forget that he'd leave.

"Well, Sundays are normally a take-it-easy day. I've fed and watered all the animals we keep close by—the chooks, dogs, horses—and I've mucked out the coop and the stable. I normally go for a ride on Tilly. If you want, you can come too."

"Yeah?"

His smile was wide and eyes bright when he asked. The bloke couldn't mask his enthusiasm if he tried. I nodded, and Pete picked up our empty plates and cups, took them to the sink, and scrubbed away at them until all the pots, pans, crockery, and cutlery were pristine and drying on the rack next to the sink.

If he caught me staring at his arse when he turned round, he didn't let on. I could have played it off as being lost in thought, but I was sure he saw the heat in my eyes as I watched him walk towards me. Discreetly adjusting myself before I stood, I hoped he didn't notice the bulge I was sporting. I couldn't help it. He was beautiful. I'd never thought of another man like that, but his pale skin and long, lean lines made me want to see more of him. All of him. It had me contemplating tearing down those walls I'd erected just to get closer to him. I cleared my throat, but my voice was still husky. "Let's go, then."

Pete watched me closely as I saddled up Tilly and loaded her saddlebags with water, snacks and a blanket. Then he helped me get Banjo ready. The horse was a beast, tall and solid, but our dappled grey gelding was a gentle giant. Nothing phased him; precisely the reason Pete was riding him. Banjo's name was an ode to *The Man from Snowy River* himself. Ma named him when we'd picked him up from the stockyards as a colt. He was supposed to be her horse, but she rarely got out to ride him nowadays. Since she'd been diagnosed with osteoporosis in her hips, Ma was afraid of getting knocked off and needing a hip replacement. So, while Pete was here, he'd be riding Banjo.

I held Banjo's reins and the stirrup as Pete lifted his leg high and hooked his foot in before hauling himself up. He managed it like a seasoned pro, rather than the relative novice he was. He'd confided the night before he'd had horse riding lessons as a kid. His ma wanted him to compete in equestrian competitions—apparently all the rage from where he was from in Sydney—but he'd pulled out, more interested in books than being outdoors. I couldn't fathom it, but he just shrugged adding he was a nerd at heart. As if that explained everything. He said he still loved books; in fact, he usually spent most of his time in front of a computer. But now he found himself yearning to be outdoors too. It was the space he said—he loved the openness—and that I understood. It wasn't just my dick talking, it was something more. I didn't know why, but I wanted to share with him that sense of comfort the desert gave me. To show him a piece of home. I wanted to show him round and spend time getting to know him. It was pointless denying it; I liked him.

I breathed in a deep lungful of desert air and closed my eyes, letting Tilly's steps rock me back and forth. The cool autumn breeze caressed my face. It was a perfect, sunny day. Cool enough to wear long sleeves, but warm enough that we didn't need coats.

"So, Tilly? How'd you come up with that?" he asked, breaking the comfortable silence.

"It's short for Matilda. It's kinda embarrassing really." I ducked my head and adjusted my hat, bracing myself for his laugh. "Named her after Heath Ledger's daughter, Matilda."

"Fan of *Batman*?"

How did I tell him that it wasn't Heath Ledger's Joker that I loved, but Patrick Verona in *10 Things I Hate About You*? I shook my head. Yeah, no. "Something like that."

We kept a steady pace as I directed the horses through the southern paddock to the dry creek. With red dirt below us and the bright blue sky above, the contrast was as brilliant as it was unending. The flat earth stretched to the horizon and beyond for hundreds of Ks. But at the same time, it varied. Gidgee trees dotted the ground, breaking the striking red with patches of blue-grey. A strand of ancient eucalypts reached up, their branches kissing the sky as they stretched towards the sun. Their roots would be deep enough to have hit moisture in the soil. It was the only way they were still thriving along the bone-dry creek bed. An eagle's cry pierced the quiet and had me looking up. I spotted its form high in the sky and pointed up, but Pete had already pinpointed it. "Wedge-tailed eagle. Wow," he murmured.

I didn't have a chance to respond. Banjo whinnied and reared up on his hind legs. Pete held the reins tight, keeping his body tucked in close to his saddle and Banjo's neck. The horse bucked hard, kicking out its back legs too, and Pete didn't stand a chance. Even a seasoned rider would've had trouble staying on while the horse tossed itself around like a bronco in a rodeo. Pete sailed off and hit the ground with a thud, his arms and legs splayed out wide. Banjo's hooves came down too close for comfort and my gut twisted. My breath caught. Fear shot through me, terror that Banjo would trample him, crushing the life from a man I'd only met, but who'd already made me lower my guard more than any other.

I reacted on instinct, herding Banjo away from Pete. Tilly would settle him if I could get them close enough. It must have been a snake that spooked the horse, but I couldn't see it now. I pulled on Tilly's reins again, and she turned on a dime, putting us between Pete and Banjo. Moving the scared horse away from both the threat and Pete. The moment Pete was safe, the second he couldn't get trampled by Banjo, I stopped thinking. I just moved. I needed to get to him. To see his green eyes sparkling bright, his smile, and that wonder he carried when he looked round. *Please, let him be okay*. But he still wasn't moving. My heart in my throat, I dismounted in a half-jump-half-fall kind of way, practically tripping over my feet to get to him. But they were leaden as I scrambled along the ground. I couldn't get there fast enough. He was barely a couple of metres away, but he might as well have been on the moon with how long it took for me to get to his side. I skidded to a stop next to him and grasped his hand, feeling his warmth seep through me. My heart stuttered when he squeezed it tight but lurched when he tried to suck in a breath and couldn't. He wheezed, the groan sounding pained. His eyes were wide, his gaze flitting round in a panic.

"You're right, Pete," I soothed. My voice was a lot calmer than the storm raging within me. "You've knocked the wind out of yourself. Just breathe. You'll be right." He focussed on me, his blue eyes locking on mine. He tried again, his pant more of a groan. "In through your nose. Nice 'n slow." I nodded, encouraging him. Willing him to hear me. To try. With my free hand, I ran it through his hair. The strands were as rich a red as the dirt he was lying on, and so soft. I ran my fingers through the short waves, trying to calm him more and secretly reassuring myself that he'd be okay if I could get him to take a few deep breaths. Pete closed his eyes and inhaled slowly. Just a small breath at first, but after a moment, he tried again, taking more air in. "That's it. You're doing good. Nice and deep." His chest rose slowly and I ran my fingers through his hair again. "Out through your mouth."

I tore my gaze away from him and looked round. The homestead was still within sight, but our isolation out here hit me hard. Where were our horses? My sat phone was in Tilly's saddlebag. My cool slipped a notch until I saw them behind us. They'd circled around, putting us between them and the snake Banjo must have seen. At least they hadn't bolted. I blew out a relieved breath when I couldn't see any sign of the snake either.

Pete did the same, breathing out slowly. I kept a hold of his hand and ran my fingers through his hair again, touching him. Needing the contact. He still had his eyes closed. How hard had he hit his head? "Pete, open your eyes for me, ba—mate. Come on." I caught myself before I'd called him babe. Thank God. My brain was frazzled but my voice calm as I encouraged him. He blinked his eyes open and dragged in another slow breath. The wheeze in his inhale had less-ened, and his body had relaxed. I wiped a smear of dirt from his cheek with my thumb, unable to stop myself from touching him more. Reassuring myself that he was okay. When Pete's breath hitched, I had to resist the temptation to gather him in my arms.

"Breathe nice and slow," I cajoled, stroking his short stubble softly. Pete's eyes drifted closed again, and he leaned into my touch, taking a much bigger and calmer breath than he had.

He tried to push up, but I stopped him. "Wait, is any-where hurting?"

"Everything hurts, but nothing more than anything else," he croaked. I didn't stop him when he pushed up so he was sitting. He was so close, but now I wasn't touching him. And I really wanted to. Pete did it for me, taking my hand again. Except that he shook it rather than held it. "Sorry," he started, but I shook my head.

"Don't apologize for coming off the horse. I've seen far more experienced riders get tossed when a horse has bucked like that."

"I dunno what happened. One minute we were riding, and the next I couldn't breathe." Pete took a slow, deep breath and let it out as I answered him.

"Snake spooked Banjo." Pete tried to scramble up off the ground, practically crawling into my lap, stopping only when I held a hand on his shoulder. "Shh," I soothed. "It's gone now. The vibration from their hooves would've scared it off."

"Fuck," he muttered, leaning into me and resting his head on my shoulder. It came as second nature to hold him. I ran my hands up and down his back and breathed him in, holding his spicy scent inside me. We must have made a hell of a picture. Two blokes sitting in the dirt, covered in dust, hugging, but I didn't want to let him go. He felt too good. He was warm and although not as built as me, still solid underneath my fingertips. His muscles were defined and I could feel them ripple as he tightened his hold on me. I couldn't stifle my moan when he turned his face, tucking it into the crook of my neck, his warm breath feathering against my skin. He stiffened and pulled away slightly and I reluctantly let him go, my arms falling by my sides. We were still close. Only a few centimetres between our noses separated us. Far closer than I would normally be to anyone, but with him, it felt too far.

"We, ah—" I cleared my throat and nodded in the direction of the homestead. "Should maybe go back. Let you lie down on a comfortable bed."

"I don't want to go back," he whispered. I turned to face him again and he was right there. I didn't know whether he leaned closer or if it was me, but our noses touched, and we breathed the same air. I shuddered as he nudged my nose with his, my brain blanking out and my breath catching when he hummed. "I want to lie in the shade on a picnic blanket."

I hadn't intended that we'd be going on a date, but maybe I subconsciously wanted it. Maybe that's why I'd packed our lunch and a blanket. I couldn't deny that the thought of it made my heart beat faster, and my pulse thud in my veins. God, I wanted that. I really did. All my reasons for hiding myself, for living a life in the closet seemed

inconsequential now. The reasons mattered. I had everything to lose. My family too. But I was tempted to risk it all.
Something told me that Pete was important. Worth it. To
me, to my future. I wasn't stupid enough to deny that my
reaction to his getting thrown off had shown me that I
cared. I'd just met him, but clearly, that didn't matter to
something inside me. Was I brave enough to do something
about it? Would I be able to keep it quiet? Would Pete put
up with being hidden? Could I even ask that of him?

I shook my head and mentally slapped myself out of my
fantasy land. I was an idiot for even thinking I could have
that kind of life.

# FIVE

## Pete

Everything hurt. Ached. My head spun and I couldn't catch my breath. But Scottie's words were like a balm to my body. I didn't have any broken bones, but I could only imagine the bruises I'd have. Then he went and mentioned a snake and I practically climbed him. It was embarrassing, but Scottie didn't push me away. He soothed me, held me while I had my freak out, and leaned in closer when I pulled away to try and give him space. Without thinking, I'd basically outed myself. Again. I hadn't said in so many words that I wanted him, but I might as well have.

I waited on tenterhooks for his reaction. He watched me quietly, like he was contemplating his answer before he broke eye contact and looked away. My gut sank and I feared I'd overstepped. That I was completely wrong. He shook his head and I knew I'd screwed up, but then he looked at me and nodded. I wasn't sure what it meant, but as long as he wasn't kicking me off his property, I was fine with backing off.

He stood up and held out a hand to me, helping me to my feet. I moved slowly, but I was okay. Shaken up and sore, I wasn't injured too badly. Scottie let out a short, sharp whistle, and his horse trotted up with the big bugger I'd been riding following closely behind. I hesitated, not sure if I wanted to get back on him, but I shouldn't have worried.

"You think you can walk to those trees over there?" Scottie asked me, pointing to the strand we'd been following the length of. They weren't far, only a couple of hundred metres away, and I was grateful for Scottie's thoughtfulness in not making me climb up and ride so soon after coming off.

"Yeah." I nodded and grasped Banjo's reins, taking them from Scottie's hand. We made our way over to the trees, and Scottie fussed around with the blanket, laying it out and making sure it was all straight and perfect before helping me sit down.

"Can you take your shirt off?" He hesitated and looked away. Swallowing, the movement of his Adam's apple in his throat caught my eye, before he added, "I need to check you're not all banged up, and clean any cuts."

"Yeah," I squeaked, and cleared my throat. "Yeah, sure." I pulled off my hat that Scottie had recovered and reached behind me to pull off my long-sleeved tee from the neckline. My T-shirt followed and I dropped them both next to me. Scottie's body heat from close behind me made me shiver as he ran his fingers through my hair, my nerve endings tingling. The sting from his fingers pressing against the sore spot on my head made me flinch and had him hissing.

"You've cut yourself." I nodded my response as I felt him shift. He had opened the small first aid kit he pulled from Banjo's saddlebag, and before I knew it, something cool and wet was gently pressed against the back of my head. "You're gonna have a headache tomorrow."

"Mmm," I agreed.

After a moment, rough hands trailed ever so gently over my shoulders and down my back. I shivered as he followed the length of my spine and sucked in a breath when he held his hand on my side. "That hurt?" he asked, concern etching his voice. I shook my head and blushed, embarrassment staining my face red. My cock, sporting a semi at his soft touch, twitched at the proximity of his voice to my ear and his hands to my hips. I was already putty in his hands, but if he moved those magical hands—strong and work-roughened but infinitely soft at the same time—down a few inches to my hips, I'd be—

"Oh, fuck," fell from my lips on a moan, as he wrapped his fingers around my hips and pressed. He let go instantly, and I dropped my head to my hands to stop myself from adjusting my iron-hard cock behind my zip.

"Pete, how much pain you in? Why didn't you tell me you were hurting?" He gripped his hat and yanked it down harder on his head, frustration radiating off him. "I need to get the doc out here to check out your hip."

"Scottie." I turned to him and grasped his wrist, revelling in his warmth and strength. "I'm not hurting. I.... You.... Fuck." I looked to the cerulean sky and blew out a breath, hoping that the blush that had crept down to my chest had waned. "Your hands felt good. I'm... I'm gay." I looked him in the eyes. I needed to see his reaction. The fist coming if that's what it was. "I'm sorry. I should have told you that before you touched me. You probably don't feel comforta-ble now, especially when I get—"

Fire burned in his eyes, but it wasn't anger I saw. It was heat. The desire I'd been enveloped in was reflected in his gaze. Our eyes locked and the breath whooshed out of my lungs. I needed him to touch me again with a desperation I'd never experienced before. He was gorgeous when he smiled, but the raw wantonness radiating from him now was scorching.

I didn't know who made the first move. It could have been me, might have been him. But when we came to-gether, sparks exploded. He wrapped his strong fingers around my nape, pulling me to him at the same time I grasped his waist and tugged him closer.

Our mouths pressed together in a tease of something far more incendiary to come. Soft lips and rough stubble had me moaning, and his warm, wet tongue snaked the length of my lower lip, a promise of entrance. When his tongue swept into my mouth meeting mine, it was as if he'd stuck me with a cattle prod. The zap of energy fired through every nerve ending. He took the lead, teasing and tasting me while I did the same. A faded hint of mint on his breath had me chasing his tongue, wanting to taste more of him.

On our knees, we shifted, pressing our bodies closer, every hard inch of him against mine. His warmth, his strength surrounded me, and I still wasn't close enough. I knocked his hat off his head, letting it fall to our side as I pulled away, licking and sucking a path down his neck. Scot-tie's hands on my shoulders tightened as he threw back his head and moaned. It was the sexiest thing I'd ever seen. Possessiveness washed over me. I wanted him to be mine, to have my mark all over him. His scent, spicy and rich, filled my nose as I buried my face into the crook of his neck and breathed deep. I wanted him inside me and all around me. I sucked the soft skin near his collarbone into my mouth and gently bit down, marking him as mine in a way I didn't have a right to do. Scottie shuddered, and I could feel the length of his hard cock even through the layers of denim from our jeans. Sharp stubble tickled my lips as I kissed up his throat again until Scottie pulled away and crashed his mouth against mine once more.

We might have kissed for seconds or hours. All I knew was that I was as hard as the timber from the eucalyptus trees we were kneeling under. I wanted more. I wanted everything, but now wasn't the time or place. One day into my stay and I'd already come out and jumped the station owner too. I pulled back reluctantly, catching my breath, and dropped my gaze to our bodies, still pressed tightly against each other. "Guess that clears up why you don't get out and meet a nice girl then," I mumbled, sitting my arse on my heels.

Scottie's laugh, deep and joyful, surprised me, and I looked back up at him. He sat, stretching his legs out in front of him and took my hand in his. The crinkles around his eyes and the dark lashes framing them made the blue of his irises stand out, and I was struck dumb by how beautiful he was. "Yeah, not really my kinda thing," he answered, and I blushed, not really sure why I was shy all of a sudden. He reached out and ran the pad of his thumb over my cheek and my skin burned with his touch. My face was aflame, my cheeks about as red as they could get. "Who knew that my type was sexy rangas?"

I ignored his backwards compliment, mainly because I couldn't blush any harder than what I was, and instead said the first thing that came into my mouth. "But your mum and nan keep hassling you to find someone?" At least I hadn't asked him outright whether he was still in the closet.

It was Scottie's turn to look away. "They don't know. No one does. You're literally the only person in hundreds of Ks who knows. I can't come out." He shook his head and sighed, the weight of the world seemingly on his shoulders. He probably felt like it was. I had no idea what it would mean for someone like him—living in the outback, a business owner who relied on local suppliers—to announce he was gay. I thought that the world was more accepting, but all it took was a look online to see the vitriol that the trolls spewed at us. And I lived in Sydney, home of Mardi Gras. Out here was worlds away from my accepting neighbourhood where half of the building I'd lived in identified as LGBTIQA+.

"Yeah, I can guess why. It must be hard feeling so alone." He went quiet and my heart broke for him. It was my turn to reach out. I shifted, sitting down next to him, our bodies touching from shoulder to thigh. Reaching for his hand again, I clasped it tightly. "I can't imagine what you've gone through keeping it a secret. Feeling like you couldn't tell anyone. For as long as I'm here though, we can talk. You don't have to hide around me."

"I…. Thank you." His voice was quiet but strong. "It's not because you're here either. I mean, I didn't just kiss you because you said you're gay and I'm desperate—" He laughed, cutting himself off with a shake of his head. "I'm totally screwing this up."

"No, you're not," I reassured him. "I understand what you're trying to say. I know I'm hot," I joked, knocking his shoulder playfully. I expected him to laugh, but when I turned to him, his eyes were filled with fire again. A molten ice blue. I moaned, and Scottie reached for me again, pulling me towards him. I went willingly, but unlike last time when our kiss was explosive, this one was softer, slower. Intimate. Our breaths mingled and our tongues tangled, learning each other's mouths.

"You're right," he murmured between kisses. When I pulled back and furrowed my brows at him, he grinned. "You are hot." I chuckled and our lips met again with us still smiling.

We stayed like that for hours. Kissing, talking, and lying on the blanket looking up at the sky. I was resting my head on his shoulder, my eyes closed as I drew random circles on his chest. "Are you happy here?" I asked, wondering whether he would ever leave even if he wasn't.

"I love this place. This land." He gently ran his fingers through my hair, playing with the strands at my nape. "I'm nothing special, but these paddocks, this desert?" I felt him shift and knew he'd held his hands out wide, gesturing around him. "It is, and it's part of me. I couldn't imagine being anywhere else but here."

"You're wrong, you know," I said, resting my chin on his arm. "I've only been here for a day, and I can already see that you're something else. Your family respects you. You're successfully and sustainably managing half-a-million hectares of land in an environment that would break most people."

"It's just what I do." He shrugged, and I shook my head, amazed he was so down to earth. He was humble, and that on a man who'd achieved so much was bloody sexy.

"It may be what you do, but it's also pretty damn impressive." I reached up and turned his chin to mine, capturing his lips again in a slow, sweet kiss. Scottie rolled me onto my back and straddled my waist, never breaking our kiss. I reached up, slipping my hands under his shirt to finally touch soft, warm skin. His muscles flexed as he held himself above me and rocked his hips. With one hand on his arse, urging him on and the other digging into the muscle of his back, I kissed him hard. Scottie reached down and ran his calloused fingers over my pebbled nubs, pinching me gently. The move had me gasping and my hips grinding into his, seeking friction on my aching dick. The reaction must have been one he liked. He pressed me harder onto the blanket and slammed his mouth against mine.

The hiss of pain I let out had him freezing above me and then clambering off. "Fuck, I'm an idiot— Your head. I'm sorry."

"I'm okay. Really. Just get back here." I sat up and pulled him to me again, but he didn't press his lips to mine, instead resting our foreheads together for a moment. Running his hands up and down my sides, he looked at me and smiled softly.

"Your freckles don't cover all of you," he said, wonder in his voice as he traced the point on my chest where the freckles faded to reveal my pale skin. Then he followed the line between my pecs down to my happy trail. There was no doubting I was a natural ginger—the red line of hair connecting my belly button to my pubes was a dead giveaway. "Your skin is perfect."

"Hardly." I huffed. "But I'll take the compliment." His eyes were following his hands as he smoothed them over my sides and moved one up to finger my collarbone.

He groaned and lifted off me. I saw the shift in his expression and knew that our day together was coming to a close. "The others will be wondering where we are. They'll be back by now."

"S'pose we should head back then?" It was a rhetorical question. The last thing I wanted was for one of Scottie's hands to spy the horses and come and check on us. Finding me half-dressed and Scottie on top of me would be a hell of a coming out that he just didn't want.

He nodded and looked at me with sadness in his eyes. "I'm sorry I can't be open. I mean, you probably don't want to announce what we were doing anyway—it's not like we've even hooked up—"

"Scottie." I tilted his chin to mine. "Let's just take this slow, yeah? You're right. I'm not ready to announce us— whatever we are—to your family, but it's not because I wouldn't be proud to hold your hand in front of them. I'm not ready to come out to everyone here either. I'm out at home, but... I've got to feel comfortable before I say something."

He nodded and leaned forward, pressing his lips to mine in a silent promise to take it easy on ourselves before he stood and held out his hand, helping me to my feet. I slid on my shirt, found my hat and folded the blanket while Scottie whistled for the horses and gave them an apple out of the container we'd had our sandwiches in. "You wanna double up with me, or will you be right to ride Banjo back?" he asked as he packed our things into the saddlebags.

"I'll be right." I petted Banjo's neck and added, "As long as we have an understanding that I won't be getting tossed off again." Scottie checked the saddle and reins and helped me get a foot in the stirrup so I could heave myself onto the big horse. He handed me the reins, and I held Banjo steady as Scottie mounted Tilly and clicked his tongue, both horses moving at his command.

"So tell me about the people you have working for you," I started after we'd turned the horses towards the homestead and begun our steady pace back.

Scottie grinned. "They're a motley bunch, but family, you know? Jono's my head stockman. He's in his early sixties. Don't call him out on it though 'cause he'll tell Ma you're calling her old and there's usually a bit of full naming after that." He huffed out a laugh when I snorted. "Craig and Sam have both worked here for nearly fifteen years, and Den about eight. Craig and Sam are two peas in a pod. They're best mates in their late thirties. They've lived together since they were teenagers. Sam's family owned a station in the early two-thousands, and Craig's dad worked there. They lost it because of the drought. They had to sell what cattle they didn't lose to the conditions and the bank foreclosed. Since then they travelled a bit, working in New South, then came home. Ma hired them as soon as she knew they were back in town. They're funny bastards. Finish each other's sentences all the time too. And Den's dad's a dogger in WA, but he couldn't do it—"

"What's a dogger?" I asked, interrupting his flow.

"Hunters that target dingoes crossbred with domestic dogs. Dingoes used to be regarded as pests and were hunted. Now people have realized it's the domesticated dogs that are the problem. They're trained to hunt and then dumped or escape. When they crossbreed with dingoes, you have big litters of pups, and they're in heat more often than dingoes, so the population explodes. They're aggressive too. Dingoes are normally solitary animals and tend to avoid populated areas, but the domestic dogs don't. The feral dogs are pests, so when they're found on stations and small livestock farms, they're culled. Den didn't wanna do that, so he struck out on his own and made his way from WA through the Territory and over to Mount Isa. Met him at a rodeo, and he decided to come back and check out the station. I hired him after that."

"Ally said you have an aboriginal couple working here too."

"Yeah, Waru and Yindi. Pops was out injured when we were doing the muster. Nan stayed here to look after him. The rest of us were all out there, and even still, we were short-handed. Waru and Yindi were visiting some of their ancestral grounds and were just walking across the paddock where we were mustering. They jumped in and helped round up a few strays on foot. Ma knew them and asked them to stay with us to do the muster. After that, they kinda just stayed. Their knowledge of these parts, their tracking abilities, and survival skills are all invaluable. They've saved our lives more than once."

"They all sound pretty special."

"They are. And they're gonna eat you for breakfast, City. Be prepared for them to take the piss out of you."

"Like hazing? Or just teasing?" I asked, my brows furrowed. If they were the hazing kind, no wonder Scottie hadn't come out. Even with the respect of his mother, grandmother, and sister, they wouldn't be enough to protect him against four, maybe five blokes who worked the land for a living. Not to mention the rifle that Scottie had strapped to Tilly's saddle. In the wrong hands, it could do some serious damage.

Scottie shook his head and uttered, "Nah, mate. Teasing only. If anyone lays a hand on someone else on this station, they're out. When Pops was in charge, there used to be drinking and fighting on a Saturday night. The boys would get rowdy. Ma hated it, but they threatened to walk if she made them go dry. Then she thought bugger it and did it anyway. We lost a few of the boys but we're better off with the people we have now."

"How long has your family been here for? Three generations is a lot of time."

"Five generations. Near on a hundred and fifty years."

"Wow. Has anyone left? Like, lived here for a bit or grew up here I suppose, then moved away?"

Scottie gave a sharp nod. "I've got two aunts who live in Brisbane now. But yeah, others have left too."

The way he said it, the finality, and the mix of anger and melancholy in his tone made me think it was someone close to him, but I didn't know who. I didn't have time to ask either. We'd rounded the homestead and were met by three of the five generations of Pearces together with two blokes who acted like twins yet were completely different at the same time, and another older man, who at a guess I'd say were Craig, Sam, and Jono.

Scottie dismounted and bumped fists with the two who seemed to move in sequence and shook hands with the other before taking Banjo's reins from me and holding him still while I slowly climbed off. It wasn't pretty. In fact, it was more of a slide and fall than actually getting off him. I stumbled and would have landed on my arse if it wasn't for the older man catching me.

"Woah there, mate." He righted me and I flushed beetroot red. His hand shot out and he added, "The name's Jono. I'm guessing you're our visitor."

I took his hand and he shook mine with a bruising grip. "Pete McKenzie, yeah."

"Nice to meet you. Okay for us to call you Macca?" When I nodded, he smiled and added, "This here is Craig and the taller one's Sam." I shook hands with both of them and looked to Scottie for direction on where we were taking the horses but didn't get a chance to ask him anything before the aboriginal couple who Ally had told me about rounded the corner.

I was introduced to them, and Yindi asked, "Where were you today, boss? See anything that needed doing?"

"Nah, didn't get that far out. Banjo got spooked and bucked Pete off. We just hung around the old creek bed for a few hours then rode back." Turning to me, he added, "You're gonna be sore tomorrow so you might want to have a hot shower."

"Not if you're buying water. I'll do the same that everyone else here does and just fill up the sink. But thanks." I motioned to the horses. "Do we need to brush them down or anything?"

Scottie looked up to the sky. "Yeah, we'll do that, then we'll need to freshen up for tea. Come on, City, let's do this."

I sat next to Scottie at the dinner table and watched, embarrassment colouring my cheeks red, as he retold the story of me trying and failing to hold on as Banjo bucked and kicked after being spooked by a snake.

"You'll have a nice egg on your noggin' tomorrow, Macca," Craig said. "Rip-roaring headache too."

"Yeah, I can already feel the lump," I replied, fingering the sensitive point at the back of my head, "I don't have too much of a headache though."

"You're lucky you didn't break something," Jono added. "Has Scottie told you the station rules? No going out alone? Something like that happens, and you're alone and—"

"You'll be on a mission to recover a body, not a rescue. Yeah, he said." I grinned. "I'm not stupid enough to think I can hack it out in the desert by myself. I've been here, what, twenty-four hours and I've already come off a horse. I can only imagine what damage I'd do to myself left unsupervised for too long."

The conversation continued, and Scottie pressed his leg against mine, hooking his foot around my own under the table. I lifted my lips in a small smile aimed just for him and I was sure he'd caught on when he brushed my socked foot with his.

After we'd done the dishes, Ally decided to watch a movie in the living room, and Craig and Sam opted to join her. Den and Jono retired to their cabin, planning to continue the chess game they were in the middle of and Waru and Yindi stayed with Ma and Nan in the kitchen with a cuppa. True to her word, Ma had found a supermarket open on a Sunday and bought one of every kind of coffee they had. Which wasn't much, but the two cups I'd restricted myself to that day were like heaven in a mug compared to the tasteless stuff I'd had that morning. Scottie boiled the kettle, making us each a hot drink and tilted his head to the door. "Wanna go sit outside?"

"Yeah."

We wandered out across the darkened space. I was expecting to take the same spots around the campfire as the night before, but instead, he led me to the guesthouse. We didn't bother turning on any lights. It was intimate just the two of us, and I couldn't help but smile. Butterflies in my belly and a grin that I couldn't wipe made me appreciate the silvery glow cast through the windows by the moon. Scottie placed a warm hand at the base of my spine and smiled at me when he led me to the door off the kitchen and held it open for me. The butterflies in my belly took flight when I saw what was outside. I was suddenly shy seeing the two-person swing, the white paint glinting in the moonlight. It was romantic and sweet, and for two grown men, it would be a cosy fit. Quiet surrounded us, the silhouettes of the buildings punctuated against the millions of pinpricks of light and a moon that was so big in the sky I could imagine reaching out to touch it. It was spectacular. "Gives new meaning to the nursery rhyme," I mused, going to stand against the post.

"Huh?" Scottie asked, clearly confused by my nonsensical comment.

"The cow jumped over the moon. From here it looks close enough to touch."

Scottie came to stand behind me and rested his forehead at my nape, wrapping an arm around me. "You don't ever get sick of it out here. I love night-time, sitting out under this Southern Cross sky.

"It's nothing like I've ever experienced before. I love it already." And it was true. The sounds of the desert—the hiss and chirp of the night insects, the odd animal call. The wide-open spaces, the darkness wrapping like a blanket around us in our little bubble of perfection on that veranda. Peace washed over me, and I couldn't help but compare it to the city. I couldn't think of a single thing I missed about being in Sydney.

Scottie took my hand in his and led me over to the swing. He sat, kicked off a shoe, and put one leg up on the seat. He had the other splayed wide and motioned for me to sit between his legs. Warmth filled my chest as he patted the seat before him and I slid into place. Scottie handed me the blanket and one-handed, I spread it over us, trying not to spill my half-full coffee mug. Wrapping his strong arm around me, he pulled me back against him and I relaxed into his embrace. He was warm and comfortable and his hold on me had me craving more of the same. When he rested his chin on my shoulder, then kissed my cheek, I signed happily. Soft cushions under me, a muscular chest behind, and the heat of the coffee in my hands had me practically purring.

"Thank you for making me feel so welcome," I murmured. "Everything about this place is special, and your family is great."

"They're good people, all of them."

"They are." Scottie lifted his mug to his lips and I asked another question. "If I wasn't here, what would you have been doing?"

"Probably watching the movie with Ally and the boys. Maybe read a book." Scottie nuzzled my nape, sending shivers down my spine. "I'm glad you're here though."

"So am I." He kissed my throat, then slow open-mouthed kisses up to my ear and goosebumps broke out over my skin. I moaned, a sound that was far too needy falling from my lips.

He nibbled on my skin and I closed my eyes, loving every moment of being in his arms. He was warmth and affection, generous with his touch. I let him explore, wanting nothing more than him to keep going as I tilted my head to the side to give him access. Scottie's rumbly hum told me he liked it and that sent another wave of warmth through me. He handed me his half-full mug and chuckled against my skin as I looked over my shoulder at him wide-eyed. How the hell was I supposed to keep them steady when he was working me over like that?

Both hands freed, he slipped them under my shirt, his rough skin against my own infinitely gentle. He was learning my body, and that sent a ripple of awareness through me. No one had ever taken the time to do that. Sure, I'd taken men home before, and we'd rolled around, but no one had taken the time to catalogue every one of my reactions like Scottie seemed to be doing. Each hum, each whispered, "Yeah," when I arched into him or shuddered, let me know he was taking it all in. When he repeated the move, sending me higher and higher as he continued to lick and suck my neck, I wanted to shed my clothes and get as close to him as I could. I wanted to make him feel every ounce as special and as cared for as he'd made me feel that day.

The warmth of his breath and lips against my throat, his hands mapping my abs, and the hardness pressing against my back had me shifting, desperate to get closer. "Oh, fuck," I moaned. It turned into a choked gasp when he palmed my cock through my jeans. Rubbing me slowly with just the right amount of pressure had me bucking into his grasp, but it wasn't enough. I needed to feel him skin on skin with a kind of desperation I'd never experienced before. Panting, my breath coming hard and fast, I whispered, "Please."

"Whaddya need, Pete?" His words in that raspy, rumbly voice of his frazzled my brain, making my neurons misfire and my body bow into his.

*Keep touching me. Keep going.* "You. Just... you." Scottie flicked open the button on my jeans, and I hissed out a "Yes."

Those seconds he took to draw the zip down were the longest of my life. I hovered in this plain of existence of pure want. But every fuzzy thought, every overwhelmed sense snapped back into fine focus when he reached inside my underwear and grasped me tight. Desire pulsed through me, drawing my balls up tight and making my arsehole clench. Damn, I wanted to feel him inside me. I wanted to be inside him. I wanted everything. I wanted to rush and dive in head first to experience everything with him. But at the same time, I never wanted it to end. I wanted to take my time with him.

Control in tatters from thinking of all the things I wanted to experience with this man, I clenched my jaw, white-knuckled the mugs, and tried not to come that instant. Working me over with slow strokes and the odd flick of his wrist brushing the head of my cock with his callused hand, I toed the edge, barely holding myself back from the point of no return. He locked his lips on my throat and, with firm strokes, jacked my cock. I gasped for air and tried to rock into his touch, but he held me in place, kept me steady with his other hand. His control, the way he played my body, was bloody sexy. Instinctively I knew I could trust him and when I handed over that trust to him, he'd make me fly.

Then he found my kryptonite again. He curled his free hand around my hip and squeezed. Just enough pressure to hit my erog zone and send me spiralling. I choked out a sound that sounded suspiciously like a grunt, and my orgasm barrelled towards me.

"That's it, babe. I wanna see you come." His low words rumbled in my ear and the touch of his hands all over me sent me over the edge. I cried out and bucked my hips as the tingling that I'd been trying to hold off since the moment he'd touched me, erupted. I shuddered as electricity passed through me, and my dick pulsed. My cum shot over his hand in thick white ropey strands. Breathing hard, I rested my head against his shoulder and twitched while he kept slowly stroking my sensitive cock, sending shocks through my system. He shifted and kissed me then, long and lazy while and he held me close.

"Gimme a minute and I'll clean us up. As soon as I can feel my legs again," I mumbled against his lips. Scottie smiled and nuzzled me, holding me as the aftershocks had passed, and the stickiness got too much. I rose and he followed me closely, warming the water from the tap while I stripped and tossed my laundry in the hamper.

"Lemme look after ya," he directed as I reached for one of the fluffy rust-coloured towels rolled up on the vanity. Taking it out of my hand, he wet it in the warm water and swiped it over me with gentle strokes. There was nothing hurried by his moves, and I couldn't resist leaning into him. As much as I wanted to kiss him and never stop, I wanted to cuddle into him just as much. As if he was reading my mind, he said, "How 'bout we get you into bed? Come on."

He tossed the towel into the hamper and led me, hand in hand, into the bedroom, pulling down the covers and waiting for me to climb in before stripping out of his jeans and slipping in behind me.

"It's my turn to look after you." I tried to roll over, reaching for him at the same time, but he stopped me with a hand on my forearm. It was gentle, and the way he cupped my arm had me looking over my shoulder at him. The sight before me made my heart skip a beat and my breath catch. I bit my lip, looking him over. His dark hair and tanned skin contrasted against the white of the sheets. Lips kiss swollen and wet like he'd just licked them made me want to lean in and kiss him again. So I did; just a soft brush of lips against his as I tried to show him how special he was.

As he sank into the pillow, his eyes closed and he smiled. His features were relaxed. No tightness around his eyes or crease in his forehead. He looked younger, but the grey at his temples revealed a life he'd already lived. I wanted to know everything about him, and his words filled me with hope as bright as beams of sunlight piercing through the clouds on a rainy day that I'd be able to do that. "Shh, we've got plenty of time for that. Close your eyes. I wanna lie with you before I have to head back."

"Wish you could stay," I mumbled, already feeling the pull of sleep with his strong arms around me, and his bigger body curled into mine.

"Yeah. Me too." He kissed my shoulder then, and sleep overtook me.

# Six

## Scottie

I didn't want to leave, but I had to. For the first time in my life, I was tempted to say bugger it and stay, consequences be damned. But I didn't. I sat, fully dressed, on the edge of the bed in the same spot I'd been in for at least twenty minutes. I was stalling. Looking my fill of the man who was lying naked and beautiful and fast asleep. I was officially a creeper.

I leaned down and pressed a kiss to his forehead before tiptoeing out to the veranda where I'd left my boots. Shaking them to dislodge any creepy crawlies, I then slipped them on and walked round the guesthouse towards the homestead. All the lights were off when I walked in, but it didn't matter. I knew every creak in the worn timber floors, where every piece of furniture was too. I made my way to my bedroom, stripped down to my undies, and fell into bed. It was cold and the mattress wasn't as comfortable as the newer one in the guesthouse. The doona wasn't as fluffy either. Or maybe it was the man lying in there who made it better. I shook my head. I'd already taken far too big a risk. Already done what I swore I wouldn't—begin anything close to home. But as much as those promises to myself weighed heavily on my mind, there was another voice telling me not to rule it out. There was one undeniable truth with Pete. He turned me inside out. Made me want things I had no right wanting.

I had an early start the next morning and a muster to get ready for. It was only a short one—we kept the cattle close given we had to run feed out to them. But keeping them in the same paddock for much more than their usual rotation damaged the land too much. Their hard hooves compacted the soil and, in places, led to erosion. There was so little food out there that leaving the cattle grazing in an area would result in it being razed, leaving nothing for the native wildlife. Part of our commitment to manage the station sustainably was to minimize the impact of our cattle on the land wherever possible, so even though we didn't like having to transport the feed further afield than the closer paddocks, we had to.

We'd be packing most of our gear tomorrow, ready to be loaded in the ute. The hands would be servicing the quadbikes and ute, and Jono would look after his baby—our R22 chopper. Ma and Nan were going to spend the day preparing the food supplies and cooking up dinner for us. Before repairing the fences, the others had turned off the pumps for the bores in the farthest corner of the paddock we were mustering from, making the water supply dwindle. The mob would've moved closer, but there were always stragglers. Jono would sort them out, bringing them down to the main herd that we'd be mustering on the ground. I sighed. I had plenty of time to think about all that tomorrow. Now I needed sleep. I pulled up the blankets and furiously tried to ignore the semi I'd been sporting since dinnertime. The feel of Pete against my chest, his hardness in my hand, the way he moaned and let go when he came, his kiss and the way he responded to my touch had driven me crazy. Made my skin tingle with need. It'd taken every ounce of strength not to jump him when he'd climbed into bed naked. Feeling his lean muscled legs pressed against mine as I spooned him was a test of my will. The way he pressed his ass into my groin and my cock slid perfectly between his cheeks, was temptation the likes of which hadn't been seen since Adam and Eve. I wasn't real sure why I'd held out, why I hadn't let him get me off, except that holding him felt good. Doing that for him felt right in the moment. I was happy to wait for my turn, even if I ended up blue-balling until it happened.

I closed my eyes and eventually drifted off, waking with a start when my body clock dinged. I hadn't had anywhere near enough sleep the last two nights, but it was low on my list of priorities at that moment. I pulled on some trackies and a jumper, then stumbled into my attached bathroom, took a leak, splashed water on my face, and brushed my teeth before going in search of a pair of socks for my frozen feet. It was a cold morning, but that was nothing new for the desert. With the air fogging up in front of me as soon as I stepped outside, I hurried into the relative warmth of the shed. I started with the horses, opening the pens and letting them walk out into the yard on their own, stopping to pet each one and giving a little more love to Tilly. She was missing our rides and so was I. I scratched her behind her ears and she nuzzled my shoulder. I hoped that meant she forgave me.

After I'd added new feed and water to the troughs outside, I went back in and mucked out the stalls, adding new straw to them. It was physically demanding work sometimes, but I loved it. There was nothing better than waking up early and seeing the fog rolling over the desert like a wave. Being the first person to greet the animals each day gave me a connection with them that I treasured. Every animal on the station played its role. Our horses were the closest things to pets we had, but even then, they got worked hard. I loved being able to reward their loyalty and say thank you by the little gestures like giving them some love each day. Those private moments were something I'd been doing for decades. I'd never wanted to share them before, but now I imagined Pete doing it with me. I wasn't sure if that scared me or made me happy.

The dogs were next and finally, the chickens. Our rooster, Derryn Hinch, was already crowing when I'd let the dogs out, but that was normal too. Hinchy was the alarm clock none of us needed. "Mornin', Hinchy," I called out, knowing it wouldn't shut the bugger up. He ruled the roost, quite literally, and took it upon himself to let every other living being in a few-kilometre radius know exactly that. Chest puffed up and feathers ruffled, he crowed and crowed.

I collected three out of every four eggs from the hens and marked the ones we were letting them raise with an X. It was a low-tech solution that meant we never accidentally cracked the wrong egg. It helped keep the size of the brood up and meant that we had a steady supply of chicken as well as beef for our meals. My overly detached attitude with the chickens was a hard-earned lesson. I'd had a favourite when I was younger. A chick that followed me around every time I walked inside the coop. She'd grown into a beautiful speckled hen that let me pet her and carry her around without ever pecking me. Ally had tried to copy me and ended up with scratch marks all down her arms and body from where the hen fought for dear life. Dad had lost his shit, demanding that the hen be that night's dinner. Poor Jono was stuck carrying out the order, and Ma had cried the whole time she plucked that bird. I'd been beside myself the whole time. It took me close to five years to touch a piece of chicken after that.

Feathers fluttered everywhere when I walked through the coop checking their bedding. The hens were used to me hanging around by now. They didn't often have a go at me, preferring instead to peck around in the dirt outside looking for the feed I'd scattered together with the veggie scraps.

I didn't need to change the bedding in the coop yet, but if I didn't do it that day, Ma would have to do it while we were mustering. So I cleaned the bedding, raking out the old straw and replacing it with a fresh supply. It would have been backbreaking work for Ma, whereas for me, it was just a pain in my arse—dirty and smelly work.

With the straw piled up ready to go, I trekked over to the main shed only to see Pete standing on his veranda watching me. The fluttering in my belly from seeing him made me smile. But even thinking about him did that. I'd woken up with a grin and it hadn't left my lips since.

"Mornin', City," I called out with a wave. He grinned at me and shook his head.

"You're too bloody cheerful for someone who got woken up by that crowing menace." He pointed over to Hinchy scratching in the dirt near the coop. I chuckled, laughing at how he was sensitive to that crap, yet horns and revving engines probably wouldn't worry him.

"You gotta wake up early here, mate." I walked over to him, so I didn't keep yelling across the yard, and added with a hitch of my thumb over my shoulder, "I was up before Hinchy."

"You named your chook Hinchy?"

"Rooster, yeah. After Derryn Hinch. Y'know the politician?"

"Yeah, but I'm trying to figure out why you'd do that."

"Pops used to listen to him crow on every night on the tele when he had his current affairs show. Nan said he was as bad as the rooster, and ever since then, all our roosters have been named Derryn Hinch." I shrugged. It was the way we named shit out here.

"You guys are strange, you know that. Good strange, but still strange."

I grinned at him, and he shot me one of those heated stares he'd given me the day before when we'd been making out under the tree. "Eh, you get used to the way things work out 'ere." I motioned to the shed. "Gotta get the tractor out and move some hay over to the compost bins. Wanna come for a ride before brekkie?"

"Sure." He smiled, kicking his socked foot out. "Lemme get my boots on." He tipped the mug up to his lips, drinking what was left in it and ducked inside, letting the screen door bang behind him before doing it again on the way out. I couldn't help my wince both times. Even as a grown man, Ma would hand me my arse if I did that. Come to think of it, she'd probably do it to Pete too.

We jogged over to the shed, needing to make quick work of the pile of droppings and straw or face Ma's wrath for being late for brekkie. "Can you move the Landcruiser and park it round the side so I can get the tractor moved? Keys are on the sun visor." I pointed to the bigger tractor. "I need the bucket or I'll be doing it manually; it'll take me hours."

"No worries." He got in the Landcruiser while I moved to the ute, and we had them out of the way and the tractor bouncing toward the chicken coop in no time. I'd raked the straw into the clearing right where the narrow door at one end of the coop was. I edged forward, getting the bucket into the opening with inches on each side to spare and climbed down.

When I hopped out, Pete followed, and he didn't hesitate to pick up the second spade I had in the bucket. We worked together, shovelling until the floor was bare dirt. I spread more of the clean straw over the cleared area and then Pete closed the coop door so the chickens couldn't escape their fenced-in home and dingoes couldn't get in.

We kept the compost bins on the other side of the veggie patch so we could easily turn the organic nourishment onto the garden. It kept Nan's veggies happy and avoided the need for any chemical fertilizers being used on the land.

Pete was standing on the step ready for me to sit in the driver seat so I could move the tractor over there when I stopped on the step on the opposite side of the tractor and asked, "You ever wanna try driving a tractor?"

"Are you kidding? Hell yeah!"

He climbed in, and I gave him a rundown of the controls before I let him have at it. He was cautious driving, taking everything slow, exactly the way he should have. He listened to my instructions and checked then double-checked his positioning before he slowed to a stop. "Okay, you'll need to lift the bucket, go forward a couple of metres and then tip it into the bin. I'll hop off and direct you. Think you can handle it, City?"

"I prefer it when you call me babe." The fire in his eyes had me sucking in a breath and leaning closer without even realizing it. He was magnetic, and I was already treading a dangerous path. All it would take was one misstep for me to fall off and ruin everything. But I sure as hell was tempted. So much so that I let my gaze dart round. There was no one there. We were alone. I finally did what I'd been itching to do since the moment I'd seen him and closed the distance between us. Soft lips and stubble hungrily met my mouth, and we kissed right there on the tractor. His silken tongue dipped into my mouth and I parried with it before I bit down gently on his bottom lip.

Between kisses, I replied, "Me too," and pulled away when I was dizzy enough that I knew I needed to suck some air into my lungs.

"I'll take city if you call me babe when we're alone. Just don't mix them up."

"Yeah." I nodded. That was exactly what I was worried about. I unclenched my hands from his flanny where I'd pulled him closer and smoothed out the creases in the check shirt. We needed to get going or the others would be finished brekkie before we even got there. As it was, we were going to be late. I jumped down and directed Pete, and he handled the tractor like a champ. After covering the bin with the black plastic tarp again, we booked it back to the big shed. "We won't bother putting everything away just yet. We've got to head inside or Ma'll give away our brekkie."

We walked in, Pete catching the door before it slammed and I shot a grin over my shoulder. "I may be city, but I'm not stupid. I know you don't let doors slam in hearing distance of mums." I chuckled as I hung our coats up and pointed to the bathroom at the end of the hall. I didn't need to look to know that everyone was already gathered round the table, or that every set of eyes was focussed on us. I swallowed back the prickling sensation I got, the suspicion that one of them would read me like a book and know that we'd been fooling around.

"You go freshen up in there and I'll use my bathroom." I didn't wait for him to reply before dashing into my room, pulling off my chicken-shit stained clothes, giving myself a quick scrub and putting on a fresh tee, and a blue and black check shirt just like the green check flannel Pete wore.

Ten minutes later, I was sitting at the table, the last to arrive for our morning meal. Pete was already deep in conversation with Waru, talking about how different the range in the distance looked at dawn and sunset. The desert was an ever-changing landscape. The blue sky, the red dirt, and the blue-grey leaves looked different depending on the time o' day, season and how wet or dry the year had been. I only caught part of the conversation, but Pete was telling Waru he was fascinated with the geological formation of the region. He had a whole lotta theories and technical knowledge about the rocks and dirt, but both Waru and Yindi's patient smiles told me that he'd get a lesson in indigenous creation soon that'd been handed down from generation to generation for a millennia. His and Yindi's dreamtime stories had kept me riveted for hours by the campfire. I took it as my cue to get us organized for that day.

"Okay," I said, loud enough that everyone knew I was about to hand down the day's tasks. "We've got a big week coming up so let's get onto it, hey? Jono, you'll be taking out the chopper tomorrow so can you please get her serviced and checked over? Craig, you help him. Refuel today so we don't need to do it in the morning. Ally and Den, can you service the quads, please? Sam, I need you to get all the camping gear organized. Waru, you look after the gear for the horses and Yindi, you're with me servicing the ute."

"What about me?" Pete asked. I was surprised he'd offered. This was a working station, but we didn't expect guests to do the grunt work. He was here to do his own thing, but then he added that he could help. That there was no way he wasn't coming with us, so he wanted to pull his own weight. I looked at him and he was serious. No hesitation in his gaze at all.

"Sorry, City, I didn't realize you wanted to come. Early mornings and no fancy coffee," I teased.

"I'll live, smart arse." Then he paused and added, "As long as I'm not gonna be in the way. I don't want to make it more dangerous for you guys."

"I'm taking the ute for the first day so you can ride with me. Then you can head back with Jono in the chopper once you've had enough. That way, you're not sleeping on the ground."

The corners of his mouth curled down and he shook his head. Obviously what I'd said was the wrong thing. His tone when he spoke was short and sharp. "Scottie, just gimme something to do today to help."

Okay, fine, if he wanted to help, he could. "If you're any good with cars, you can help me, and Yindi can help Waru. Otherwise, Waru is oiling saddles and checking the gear for the horses. You could help him if you'd prefer."

"Waru, I'm with you."

He didn't spare me another glance all morning, and I was left wondering how I'd fucked up so badly.

"Pete," I called as he walked away from me after lunch without so much as a word. "Pete," I yelled louder when he ignored me again and jogged after him as he made his way back to the stable. I reached out for his arm and nearly smashed into him when he stopped dead in his tracks and spun to face me.

"What?" he spat out, his green eyes ablaze. In that moment, I didn't know whether I wanted to kiss him until he forgave me or tell him to stop sulking like a big baby.

I did neither.

My ego needed to take a chill pill and I needed to find out exactly where I'd screwed up. "What did I say? I'm sorry, okay. I didn't mean to upset you or offend you. I..." The dirt at my feet suddenly looked interesting, and I kicked at a lone pebble. "I'm not good at this. What did I say?"

"Early mornings and no fancy coffee?" His voice rose in frustration. "No sleeping on the ground." He groaned and pulled his hat off, running his fingers through his hair. Blowing out a breath and looking up at the sky the same way I did when I was praying for some kinda patience. "Do you think I'm some kind of princess because I'm from the city? That I can't handle it?" His shoulders sagged and the disappointment showed in his eyes. "I may not have done a muster before, but I can survive for a few days without luxuries if that's what you're worried about. If it's a safety issue, fine. But if not, stop treating me like a... a—"

"A guest who's under no obligation to come here and work? A guest who I assumed might wanna relax after coming off his horse yesterday?" Then it dawned on me. "A..." I hesitated. What did I call him? We weren't even close to being boyfriends or partners. I shook my head and got back on track. "A man who's important to me and who I still haven't asked how he's feeling. Fuck." I rubbed my forehead. "I'm sorry. I've got shit on my mind and I didn't even think to ask. How is your head? How are you feelin'?"

"Head's a little sore to touch, but I'm fine otherwise. Look, I'm not upset because you didn't ask me how I was doing. I'm pissed because it sounded like you were assuming I was the weak city boy who wouldn't want to get his hands dirty."

I motioned to the stable and we walked inside silently. Waru wasn't in there thankfully, so I tugged on Pete's sleeve and guided him into one of the darkened corners. Cupping his face, I brushed my thumbs over his cheeks, following his cheekbone, and leaned in to kiss him slowly. A gentle brush of lips against his. A tease for me just as much as a promise to him. "I was inconsiderate and stupid." Each of my sentences was punctuated with a soft kiss that begged him for forgiveness as much as I tried to tell him I liked him. "I should've asked you what you wanted before assuming I knew. Dad never once came out on a muster. He'd stand on the step of the house in his chinos and house slippers or whatever the fuck he wore everywhere and watch us ride off. I was wrong to lump you with him. But I do need you safe; I have a responsibility to you and the others. Will you come with me in the ute and see how you go?" I brushed my lips over his once more and nudged his nose with mine, pressing him against the cold corrugated iron of the shed walls.

"Hmm?" he asked, eyes glazed over and kiss drunk. Sexy and completely focussed on what I was doing to him. I chuckled, and it snapped him out of his haze.

"Come with you in the ute. Yeah. Um, yeah." He cleared his throat and added, "I want a swag too if you have a spare one. I want to lie there at night and see the sky filled with stars." We were breathing each other's air, leaning close enough that we could whisper so when he spoke again, I had to pull back to see him properly. "I can ride a quad. I'm good with motorbikes. I could ride that if you don't want me on a horse or if you weren't taking Banjo."

"Nah, we won't take Banjo. Hasn't done enough long-distance riding of late. It'd stress him too much. But yeah, if you're good with bikes, then maybe we could swap with the boys. Give them the ute and we could ride together."

"Macca, you in here, mate?" Waru called, making me jump like a bloody roo. Pete walked halfway across the old shed before he answered, giving me time to slip on out the side door. I grinned as I crept out, then strode towards the main shed with a spring in my step.

By the end of the day, I was wrecked. My hands were filthy from grease and oil changes and fixing a buggered part of the ute's suspension. If it wasn't for Yindi and her talent for repairing anything mechanical, I would have been out there half the night. At least I was sitting at the dinner table eating my reheated homemade chunky steak pie, mushy peas, and gravy only two hours later than everyone else. Everyone going on the muster tomorrow was in bed already, getting an early night before the long ride the next day. At least mine and Pete's ride wouldn't be as rough as guts anymore after fixing the ute.

"You all set now?" Ma asked. She handed me a cuppa, and next to it set down a scone, already heaped with jam and cream, ready for me to eat once I'd demolished the plate of food in front of me.

I nodded, swallowed my mouthful, and explained, "Yeah, think so. Did all the repairs and loaded everything into the ute before I came in. Quads, horses, and chopper are all set. Just got to add lunch and we'll be right."

"You still want me to get Jono to drop tea off to you at the campsite after he comes back to refuel? While he's there, he can pick up Pete and bring him back."

"I don't think he'll come back, Ma. Told me he wants to sleep out there with us." I sighed and continued, carefully picking my words, "He's stronger than I gave him credit for." I pushed the food around my plate, hoping I hadn't revealed too much. I was good with secrets, but I had a feeling that he'd be one secret I couldn't keep. Wouldn't matter once he left, but while he was here, I needed to watch every word coming out of my mouth.

She hummed a response and I raised an eyebrow at her, silently questioning what she meant. "Not all city folk are like your dad, Scottie. He's got this look of wonder as he walks around, not boredom. He wants to be here."

"Dunno if it'll last, but that's up to him," I mumbled, sending up a mental prayer to delay that day as long as possible. It wasn't just the secret touches or the possibility of getting off that drew me to him. He and I clicked straight away, despite the age gap between us. It'd taken one conversation by the fire, and I'd been intrigued, enough that I wanted to spend more time with him. Then when he'd come off his horse, I'd near on shit a brick. I cared. And that was, perhaps, the scariest part about this whole thing. Hook-ups in random bars on my twice-yearly visits to Brisbane and Sydney rarely even involved names. Rarer still were they repeats. But I wanted to get to know Pete. He had an adventurous spirit in among the book smarts. That spirit was one I recognized all too well in myself. One that would suit him perfectly if he stayed here.

If only.

I could dream, right?

"Righteo, I'm off to bed," Ma said, snapping me out of my daydream. "G'night, hon. Sing out if you need anything."

"I'll be right, Ma. Thanks for dinner."

"Leave your dishes. I'll tidy up in the morning. You go get some shut-eye." She leaned down and kissed me on the cheek and I hugged her tight for a moment. Ma was the backbone of this place. You wanted to know something— whether it was the most humane way to brand cattle, how to birth a calf when the cow's in distress, or the best off-road tyres to use on the ute—you went to Ma. Between her and Nan, they were the nurses, the educators, the office managers, and the cooks. Without both of them, I'd be lost. I didn't give either one nearly enough love for that.

I savoured the fresh baked scone while I debated whether to fall exhausted into bed or to stop over at the guesthouse before I hit the hay. It really was no competition. I wanted to see him. To say goodnight. I knew before I'd even finished the first half that I'd be out the door the moment I had my plate in the sink.

The soft creak of the door opening caught my attention, and I grinned as Pete walked in. Without a word, he motioned up the hall and I responded, "Ma's just gone to bed. Nan and Ally are both asleep."

"You'll have to be quiet then, won't you?"

Heat washed over me, but it was followed with a bucket of iced water. There was no way I was having sex—of any kind—in the house where Nan, Ma, and Ally were. I shook my head and went to protest, but Pete shushed me with a finger over his lips and sauntered out the kitchen. I don't think I've ever scoffed a scone and sculled a cuppa so fast before in my life. I wanted to toss the bloody plate at the sink, but I knew better than that. So, after placing the dirty dishes in there as quietly as I could, I dodged the creaky floorboard near the couch and practically raced into the bedroom. I was expecting Pete splayed out naked on the bed and was kinda disappointed when he wasn't, but relieved at the same time. I could only imagine how sexy he'd be with the warm light from the bedside lamp reflecting off his pale skin.

"Pete," I whispered.

"I want to taste you, Scottie." His words lit a smoulder-ing fire in me that made my will crumble. I was in the closet, not stupid, and when the man I'd been lusting over from the second I saw him sitting at our kitchen table told me he wanted me, I wouldn't—couldn't—say no. He saw the mo-ment my resolve cracked, and the scorching look he gave me made me weak in the knees.

They were all the words he uttered before he got up off the bed, stalked towards me, and reached behind my back, quietly closing the door. Then he kissed me. Soft lips against mine, his five o'clock shadow tickling the sensitive skin on my face. Stealing my breath and making me lose my ever-loving mind. Long and slow and deep, he kissed me until my toes were curling in my socks, and all the blood had rushed to parts of me that were now throbbing. He tasted sweet and smelled so damn good that I couldn't get enough. I had my hands under his jumper, feeling the muscles in his back ripple as he untucked and unbuttoned my shirt far too slowly. I wanted to bat away his hands and do it faster when he took his time flicking open the button on my Wranglers. But I resisted. Something told me he'd slow the pace even more if I tried to hurry him on.

"Pete," I choked out when he slipped his hand over my undies and palmed my cock, his other hand planted low on my back as he sucked another mark on my collarbone.

He pulled back, looking like he was gonna say something but stopped when I rolled my hips into his hand. His nostrils flared, and I did it again, then moaned when he squeezed me tight. My choked-out cry of frustration when he let me go completely was louder than I thought it'd be, but it lit a fire in Pete's eyes. His green irises glowed like emeralds, and his pupils were blown. Wet, kiss-swollen lips and the lust written all over his face made him look like an angel— one who'd been thoroughly debauched.

Pre-cum leaked from my dick, leaving a wet patch on my grey undies. I would have been embarrassed if Pete didn't see it and moan, rubbing his thumb over the spot. "Fuck, that's sexy."

He hooked a finger under the waistband of my jocks and took a step towards my en suite bathroom. I was glad he was stopping to give me a chance to clean up. I was all sweaty, and even though I'd washed my hands for tea, I hadn't cleaned the important bits—bits I was hoping with everything in me that he'd get intimate with. He warmed the water in a bucket while I stripped out of my clothes. Standing there naked in front of him, all I could think of was doing the same to Pete. I wanted to feel every inch of his body tangled round mine, but when I went to reach for him, he shook his head.

"This'll be over a shitload quicker than I want it to be if you touch me just yet, Scottie," he warned. I grinned and smoothed my hand over his arse, squeezing the thick globe.

He spun around, biting down on that plump bottom lip of his as he gripped my shoulders and guided me towards the shower. Pulling the curtain back, he manoeuvred me so I was pressed against the tile, the cold a startling contrast to the heat emanating from him. Rough jeans against my bare skin and a soft flannel shirt had me reeling. His smell, his touch—all strong and impatient made me shiver. "Stay," he directed, holding his hand up in a stopping motion.

I reached for my cock, squeezing it at the base to calm it the hell down, then reached for my balls, pulling them away from my body. My eyes drifted closed as I let my head fall back against the tile with a thunk and slowly jacked myself. "Keep doing that," Pete ground out as he carried the bucket over to us and dropped it at our feet.

I heard swishing, and when he leaned closer this time, it was his skin and the soft hairs on his legs that brushed against my own rather than the clothes he'd shucked. I sucked in a breath and opened my eyes, wanting desperately to see him. Freckles dotted his face, throat, shoulders, and arms, but otherwise, his skin was pale and flawless, milk-white like porcelain. I wanted to taste him. To lick every inch of his body and see whether that skin was as delicious as it looked. Knowing I'd had my hands on him, had touched him, had my desire ramping up higher. The natural curve in his pecs was gorgeous. Without a lot of definition, he was clearly not one that spent hours in the gym every week and I was glad for that. If I could draw my perfect man, the man who turned me on more than any other, it would have been him. Mostly flat stomach and strong legs, and in between a line of darker auburn hair leading from his navel to a flushed cock, hard and leaking.

I fought my eyes from sliding closed, my lids hooding as I watched him. He reached for my loofah sponge and dipped it in the water, bringing it up to my shoulder. The warmth against my skin made me sigh, which turned into another moan when Pete's body pressed against mine. I reached for him, hooking a hand round his nape and pulling him as close as I could get him. It wasn't enough though. I kissed him, our mouths crashing together and tongues tangling in a dance I couldn't get enough of.

My hands were acting as if they had a mind of their own, mapping the smooth skin of his chest and back. I wanted more. I wanted to touch and taste every part of him. I moved my hands to his arse, the soft hairs there making me moan. Fuck, I loved that. Loved the masculinity, the sheer maleness of a generous handful of hairy arse. Gripping him, encouraging him to grind against me, he did, and I nearly came on the spot. His hardness rubbed against mine, pressing into my belly and making me gasp. I was leaking all over the place, my balls drawn up tight against my body. Primed, I was ready to let go and sink into oblivion with him.

But then he was gone.

He pulled back, stepping away from me and I growled in frustration. I was riding the edge and he'd pushed me back rather than pulling me forward. I cracked open my eyes and watched him concentrating on his task. Soaping up the sponge and running it over my shoulders, down my arms, and over my chest, taking care of every inch of me.

"Lift your arms, Scottie," he whispered against my throat, before licking a line up to my earlobe and biting down gently. Gripping my wrists, he crossed them above my head and held them there while he ran the sponge down to my armpits and washed away the sweat and grime from the day. More water, more soap, more grinding as he washed my front, avoiding the one place I wanted him. Finally, *finally*, he squeezed the body wash onto his hand and gripped my length. Slowly, he moved up and down, working up a lather over my sensitive shaft, while he moved his other to play with the fur on my chest. "Fuck, you're sexier than I ever imagined," he mumbled against my skin as he leaned closer and took both our cocks in hand.

I gasped, my head slamming against the tiles as I held his head against my throat and arched into his touch. "Fuck, I'm close," I gritted out, but again he stepped back. "No," I cried.

"Shh," he hissed with a laugh. "If you want to keep this between us, you've got to be a little quieter."

"Bugger quiet. I wanna come."

He hummed against my Adam's apple and thrust his tongue in the hollow at the base of my throat before running it along my collarbone. "I need to wash the back of you first."

"Fuck," I groaned, shuddering in his grip.

"Turn around, Scottie." His voice was like gravel, deep and rough as he manhandled me. And damn did I love it. The feel of his hands gripping my hips, turning me, pushing my arms up above my head again, so I was pressed against the tile with my arse sticking out. He nudged a knee between my legs, and I spread them further, wanting nothing more than his hands on me again. Pete plastered his body against mine, his hard cock nestled between my arse cheeks and I flat out whimpered. Bit down on my lip when he rocked his hips forward and ground against me. Clamped a hand around the base of my cock to stop myself losing my load when he curled his fingers round my hips and bit down on my shoulder.

"God damn, you're a tease, Pete," I groaned. My words seemed to kick him into action, and he pulled away, pressing the sponge against my shoulders and latherin' me up. Down my back and over the curve of my arse, pausing like he didn't want to let go. I thrust back against him, wanting—needing—friction and Pete went back to tormenting me. He dropped to his knees and bit me. Teeth scraping against my skin had never felt so damn erotic. My breath left me in a rush and my pucker fluttered, my whole body screaming for him to move his mouth a few inches to the left. Instead, he ran the sponge down my legs and over my feet before he rose again, plastering himself behind me once more. Wet and all soaped up, we slid against each other as Pete rocked his hips into mine. When he pulled back a touch, I shot my arm back to grip his thigh and hold him in place, but I didn't think he was planning on going anywhere. His fingers played with the skin along my spine, dancing down until he reached my arse. Pulling apart my cheeks, he brushed his fingertip over my hole and a full-body shudder had me white-knuckling the tiles with my free hand to stop myself from impaling myself on his fingers. My breaths, coming in short pants, and the tilt of my hips to meet his searching fingers would have left him in no doubt what I wanted.

"Won't you be too sore tomorrow?"

"I need you inside me. Now, Pete," I begged shamelessly. He'd driven me beyond reason, beyond an ability to think clearly into the realm of instinct. And right then, the only instinct working its way through me was the one to fuck. Hard. With abandon. Banging headboards and shouted releases. "Please."

He rested his forehead against my nape and smoothed his hand down my side, dropping a gentle kiss on my spine. "Don't move, I want you exactly like this." He pulled away from me then and a moment later, I heard shuffling around in my bedside table drawers.

He pressed the lube into my hand, draped his body around mine and nuzzled my nape again. "You got a toy I can use instead?" The disappointment in his voice slayed me, and I realized there were no condoms in the drawer where I kept the lube. Why would there be? Never in my wildest dreams did I imagine ever meeting someone like him. Someone who not only was as attractive as hell, but who got me too. Who I craved. Who was here on the station with me.

"Suitcase in the wardrobe. Try the side pocket. They might be in there."

Pete stepped back, and I reached for the bucket. I didn't wanna be covered in soap when he came back. The bed was right there, and I would've loved to be in it then, tangling in the sheets with him, but I didn't think I could walk. I was so hard I was seeing cross-eyed. I picked up the water and emptied half of it over my head, rinsing away the soap before shaking my wet hair out. Waiting. Wishing he'd hurry.

# SEVEN

## Pete

I opened the cupboard doors and rummaged through his things, finding the suitcase he spoke of. Standing there naked and dripping wet in his bedroom as hard as a fence paling, I wished like hell that he had some condoms. I could have kicked myself for not bringing any. I literally had none. Not a single one. Sure, we could do almost anything else, but standing in that shower with him, soaping him up was the most sensuous thing I'd ever witnessed. I sighed, disappointment coursing through me as I pulled the duffel out of this cupboard so I could get to the side pocket. Unzipping it, I reached in, looking for the toys he kept, but I didn't find any. Instead, my fingers closed around foil wrappers. Condom-sized ones. I almost wept for joy.

Tossing a handful on the bed to take with me later, I snagged one and rushed back into the bathroom to come face to face with the sexiest sight on the planet. Scottie stood there, his skin soapy and gleaming in the low light coming from the lamps over the mirror. He held a bucket raised over his head, his face tipped back, and eyes closed. His muscles bulged, and I couldn't help licking my lips. God damn, he was beautiful. Every inch of his body was sculpted from hard work and healthy living. I wished I was recording the moment when I watched the water spill onto him and wash away the soap I'd applied to his skin. He was magnificent.

Watching him was like finding an oasis in the desert. Rare and precious. I wanted nothing more than to worship him. To bury myself in him and take him to heaven. I moaned when he shook the water out of his hair, rivulets flowing down his back and dripping onto the tiles at his feet. He turned to watch me approach and even though I was the one moving, I felt like I was being stalked. Preyed upon. His eyes on me made heat travel through my veins and my dick throb.

"Get over here, Pete," Scottie ordered, his voice deep and throaty, and his hand on his flushed cock. He reached for the lube he'd stashed on the shelf and handed it to me when I stepped back into the stall with him, before moving back into the same position he was in before—hands splayed wide against the tiled surface, face and chest pressed against it too. His legs spread, his arse begging for my touch.

"Sexiest sight I've ever seen, Scottie." I smoothed my hand down his flank and spread his cheeks open wanting to have my mouth on him. I kissed a line down his spine to his arse and swirled my tongue around, licking ever closer to his pucker. It clenched, and my blood pressure shot through the roof, lust zinging around in me. My tongue brushed against the hairs around his hole and I moaned, getting my first real taste of him. Clean and fresh and something uniquely Scottie. I wanted to savour him, to take my time and taste and tease him until he was mindless with lust, but his frustrated mewl and the uncontrollable rock of hips against my tongue told me he was already there.

I squirted lube on my fingers and prepared him, first with one finger then a second. But Scottie didn't let me go slow. There were only a couple of slow pumps of my finger to the first knuckle before he was pushing back, wanting and needing more. I went deeper, added another finger, and he was riding them, his breath choppy and his cock so hard it could hammer nails. All I could do was watch my fingers disappear and beg my cock to hold on until I was inside him to blow. "Pete," he groaned, his voice full of need and impatience. "I've been round the block before. Get in me, will ya?"

"Yeah," I rasped, suddenly jealous of the nameless and faceless men he was referring to. Getting to my feet again, I rolled on the condom, slicked up, then caged him in, running my hands down his sides and kissing the skin on his shoulders. I gripped my cock, lining it up with his pucker, and pressed forward gently, breaching him slowly. Tight heat closed around my overexcited dick, and I pushed past his resistance and paused there, trying to get myself under control. I had to hold onto him, my fingertips digging into his hips as I tried to keep steady. Scottie didn't pause, he didn't give me a chance to get myself under control, instead pushing back, impaling himself on me. I hissed, a full-body shudder passing through me, which set off a chain reaction in Scottie. He moaned and pushed back further, topping me from the bottom. And hell if I didn't love it. He knew what he wanted, and he damn well got it.

Trailing my hands up his sides, tracing the muscles there, I hooked his arm over my shoulder and turned his face to mine, needing his kiss in that moment. Needing to be connected to him in every way possible. I was inside him, wrapped around him, and I still wasn't close enough. I wanted to breathe him in, to become a part of him in every possible way. His strong body went pliant in mine as I took his lips in a kiss full of tongue and clashing teeth, nibbling on lips and shared breaths. I ground against him, pushing in further and never wanting to pull out. I could feel his heart racing under the hand I had pressed against his chest. Its tempo matched mine. Thundering through my veins as I made love to the man in front of me. His back to my chest, my legs bracketing his and my arms holding him tight, our lips joined. Me inside him as I pumped slowly in and out. Skimming my hand down his flat belly, I reached the springy curls at the base of his cock and scratched against them with blunt fingernails. Fuck, I loved that about him. He was unapologetically himself, yet at the same time, a completely different person inside to what he let others see. He'd entrusted me with that man on the inside and I felt like one of a privileged few. We'd known each other for a single heartbeat in the lifetime of this land, but we'd opened up to each other. Talked and become friends. He'd let me into his body and maybe one day, into his heart. Because I knew that this was no ordinary man. As soon as I'd seen this station on the map, as soon as I'd known its name, there was something pulling me here. I thought it was the reef, but it wasn't. It was Scottie.

I closed my hand around his cock, and that was all it took to set him off. He moaned into my mouth as his arse tightened impossibly around my dick and his own twitched in my hand, his cum pulsing out in spurts over my fist. I didn't have a hope in resisting. Scottie's orgasm was like a siren's call to my own, drawing it out of me as I held him tighter. Our kisses changed then, going from high intensity to slow and lazy. Sated. I tried to show him what he'd come to mean to me in such a short time together.

My legs were like jelly, and if there was any water left in the bucket, it had long turned cold. I pulled out of him and slipped off the condom, tying it and tossing it in the direction of the rubbish bin he had next to the toilet. Dragging the towel off the rail, I wrapped it around Scottie's shoulders and massaged his arms, drying his already dry skin. He pulled me close, pressing his forehead against mine and nuzzling our noses. Brushing his lips against mine, he wrapped the towel around my shoulders too and deepened our kiss. Stumbling back towards the bedroom, he steered me to his bed and we collapsed there, giggling like teenagers when we landed on the mattress and bounced. A dark blue feather-down doona lay neatly spread across the double bed and after we'd shifted up to lay our heads on the pillows, I tugged off Scottie's towel and pulled the covers over us as far as they'd reach. It was awkward—we were on top of the covers rather than underneath them, but I didn't want to let him go to change things up. When Scottie rolled on top of me and I spread my legs, cradling him there, he moaned softly. "You only top?" he asked between kisses.

"Vers," I breathed. "Don't bottom often, but love it when I do."

"Mmm," Scottie hummed, diving back in to kiss me harder. "I'll hold you to that." I knew he wouldn't take me that night. Even without the words being spoken, he'd be worried about my discomfort on the muster the following day. It wasn't like we were going to be on saddles, but bouncing around in the ute all day wouldn't exactly be a pleasant trip with a well-used arse. A pang of guilt ripped through me, and either he was a mind reader or he picked up on my reaction. "I wanted this, Pete. I needed you inside me and I feel fan-fuckin'-tastic. I wanted to feel you in the morning. Needed that reminder."

"I get it, but I don't want you to be hurting." I trailed my fingertips down his cheek, the stubble soft on my fingertips. I couldn't help but touch him, running the beginnings of his beard against my skin. Resting his weight on his elbows and pressing himself into me, I loved having him against me. He leaned down and kissed me again, slow and sleepy like. When he moved his lips to my throat and finally rested his head on my shoulder, I knew it was time to move. His body was shutting down for the night, and I needed to be scarce come morning. I wouldn't risk outing Scottie by being seen creeping out of his bed in the daylight hours. At least in the dark of night, I could slip out unnoticed. I rolled him to the side and kissed him again. He didn't once open his eyes, but he was still awake. Even though he grumbled about not wanting to let me go, we both knew I had to.

I dressed and covered a now-sleeping Scottie properly, kissing his temple before stealing out of his room. The creak of the floorboard underfoot had me freezing, hoping I didn't wake anyone. But when the house remained silent, I kept going, closing the door to the kitchen with a snick and jogging across the darkened dusty yard to my own bed in the guesthouse. The flannel sheets were soft but cold to the touch, and even in long pyjamas and socks, it still took some time to get warm. It was so unlike Scottie's bedroom, but even still, it was homely in a way that my room in the apartment I'd shared with Phoenix had never been. I wished I'd thought to light the fire in the stone fireplace. I hadn't in my rush to get back to Scottie, and I wouldn't change it for the world, but a little warmth in the guesthouse wouldn't have gone astray.

I lay awake for long hours mulling over how Byron's gold had brought me to Pearce Station and what was keeping me there now. I was looking forward to mustering. It was something I never thought I'd experience. Had never even thought about wanting to do it, but now? Three days in the outback had transformed my perspective. I wanted to experience everything. I wanted to learn and absorb and get to know every aspect of this station. Of Scottie. I couldn't deny my motivation lay with him. But it wasn't him alone. This land was awe-inspiring. I felt like I was part of something so much bigger. I was insignificant in this desert—a grain of the sandy dirt among its endless flat plains, but a part nevertheless. I was probably being ridiculous. Hell, the part I was playing was so insignificant that it wouldn't matter if I was there or not. I was literally tagging along. Being babysat, rather than being left to my own devices at the guesthouse. Scottie had told me about some of their other guests—artists and writers, musicians, and a researcher all using the guesthouse as their base. But not me. My base should have been a couple of hours drive north-west of the homestead in the open desert. In a quartz reef searching for gold. I should get out there. But I didn't know how to approach it. Scottie had set out their rules on day one, telling me I wasn't to go into the desert alone. I'd come prepared with camping gear and enough tinned provisions to last a couple of weeks. Water would be scarce, but I'd managed to get a big tank to fit in the tray of the ute and I had a smaller ten-litre container I could keep with me. Then I supposed I got the tiniest taste of how unpredictable things could get with a wayward snake and a horse who didn't like getting too close to it. It wasn't like he could actually stop me going. I was, after all, legally entitled to be there. Thing was, I didn't want to leave.

I tossed and turned, trying to think through my predicament. I had three months at Pearce Station. After that, I'd be broke. I either had to strike it rich or go find a real job. But it wasn't my money worries looming over me. It was the clock. It was the ever-shortening number of hours that I had left here on this station with Scottie. Truthfully, I should have already been at the coordinates where I thought the reef was, and now I was putting it off for another week. But it was a week I would get to spend sleeping outdoors under the most brilliant sky I'd ever seen. With Scottie. We couldn't be together, but he'd be near me, and that was enough. I'd get to see him in action, in his element. I'd get to know the spectacular man I'd made love to earlier that night. A smile tilted my lips as they tingled from his touch. It was better than I'd ever imagined. I only hoped there would be a repeat.

Finally, I gave up trying to sleep. Slipping on a hoodie, I padded out to the kitchen and put the kettle on the boil, but then thought better of it. Coffee at three in the morning wasn't the greatest idea. I pulled the Milo tin out of the cupboard, and warmed some milk instead, making a cup of the steaming chocolatey drink. It was sweet and warm, and I grasped the mug between cold hands and sipped it down, blowing the steam away before each mouthful.

The shadow in the yard caught my eye, and I squinted in the dim light trying to make out who or what it was. The clouds must have parted, flooding the yard in silvery moonlight, and it was then that I saw him. Scottie. Dressed in trackies and a heavy woollen jumper that looked as soft as down to touch and boots. He was a sight for sore eyes. If I wasn't as awake, I would have thought I was dreaming. But he was definitely real.

Depositing the mug on the kitchen bench, I jogged outside to meet him, the screen door slamming as I pushed through it. The cool red sandy dirt squished between my toes as I stopped close to him, closing my fists around his jumper and pulling him to me. Scottie's arms wrapped around my waist and smiled. "You should be asleep," he mused, grinning. "Or at least not outside just wearing PJs."

I had the same loopy grin on my face when I responded, "Pot meet kettle. Actually, I just boiled it. You want a cuppa?"

"Mmm, love one." With his arm still around me, warding off the chill in the pre-dawn air, we made our way inside. He pressed himself against me, his front to my back, nuzzling my nape as I made him a mug of Milo. "Wanna take this to bed?" he asked, kissing a line up my throat.

No words were needed. I grasped his jumper with my free hand, my mug in the other, and led him through to the bedroom. He'd kicked off his boots inside the door, and him standing there in my room, all bare feet and sexy had me humming my appreciation. I slipped my mug onto the bedside table and walked my fingers under his jumper. I was expecting a tee underneath, but when I found hard abs and warm skin, I leaned in and kissed him. Cool lips, his hot body, and a soft bed.

This time when we rocked against each other until we spilled onto our bellies, it was all slow hands and tangled limbs and long, lazy kisses.

The ute flew over the bumpy paddocks, Scottie expertly navigating the wombat burrows, rocks, and bushes that would have put it out of commission until we could change a tyre or fix the suspension, whichever we blew out first. The cattle were moving together, lazily walking across the desert plains. Or maybe that was Scottie keeping them in train. He revved the engine and zipped out, directing the stray cows back into the mob. He had the vehicle turning on a ten-cent piece, and suddenly, I really wanted to see him on horseback.

"How come you didn't bring Tilly?"

"Wanted to be able to ride with you." He shot a glance my way and smiled.

"So looks like I need to improve my riding skills before the next muster, hey?" I said it without thinking, but as soon as I had, I realized two things: first, I wouldn't be there for the next muster, and secondly, I really wanted to be.

Scottie took his eyes off the bumpy ground in front of us and turned to me but didn't say anything. I couldn't read his expression; in that moment, he would have made a great poker player. "Yeah," he eventually said, a shy smile tilting his lips up. "I'd like that."

We stopped for sangas at lunch. Fresh baked bread and a slathering of butter—the real stuff—corn relish and slices of roasted beef. I poured steaming tea from the thermoses we carried into waiting cups, and the hands happily drank them down. Scottie excused himself, brushing past me as he went back over to where the ute was parked and pulled a smaller thermos from behind his seat. When he handed it to me and smiled, I knew he'd made it just for me. My belly flip-flopped. A flush crawled over my face, my cheeks heating in embarrassment as I thanked him. My smile back was shy. I looked down, hiding from the curious gazes I felt on me.

The autumn sun warmed my bones as I stretched out the kinks in my back from sitting in the ute as we bounced around the desert. The breeze was cool and the cloudless sky a vibrant cornflower blue. I looked around, taking in my surroundings. The cows were mostly a faded gold, their thick legs stained red from the dust the mob threw up. They were beautiful animals—big and strong. Bred for the harsh climate and conditions. Scottie and his stockmen had worked together to bring them close to the bore, keeping them calm and watered while we stopped. The horses and dogs rested nearby, enjoying their own break under a small strand of trees that weren't much more than tall bushes. We were situated under a lone eucalypt. Its tall branches towered above us, and the thick trunk hinted at just how old the majestic tree likely was. I reached up to one of the low hanging branches and plucked off a leaf, crushing it in my hand while I waved off the flies with the other. Immediately the pungent smell of eucalyptus hit my nose and memories of childhood colds hit me. Mum would hear us sniffle and she'd have the eucalyptus oil under our noses in an instant.

Ally pointed to the branches and asked, "Grab me a few?" I pulled a handful of leaves off the closest twig and passed them to her. She crunched them up and handed them to me. "Rub them on your face and keep a few in your pocket. Helps keep the flies away." And it did. She shook her head at my delighted smile and muttered, "Newbie," with a grin as she made her way back into the shade.

Before we headed off, Scottie wandered over to the dogs and horses, petting each of them and checking them over before inspecting a few of the cows. He didn't hesitate to approach any of them, and I marvelled at how comfortable he was among his animals. "They're the best beef round these parts, and it's because Scottie's so good with 'em. Bloody good-looking animals, aren't they," Craig said. It was the first time he'd really spoken to me and when I nodded, I looked him over. He and his friend were complete opposites. Where Craig was blond, Sam had dark brown hair. Craig was stockier—thicker muscles and a shorter frame, whereas Sam was tall and wiry and yet, they were so similar. As if they could read each other's minds. They finished each other's sentences and communicated with barely a look between them. I'd seen it a few times over the last couple of days. They'd simply glance at each other and read the other's movements, inserting themselves into the exact spot the other needed. It was pretty amazing to watch how in sync they were.

"They're beautiful animals. Big buggers too," I mused.

"Yup. Gotta be careful being near them. They have a helluva kick, and they'll trample you if you're on the ground." Craig took off his hat and wiped the sweat off his brow with his sleeve, leaving a streak of red dust smeared across his forehead. "You got this to look forward to tomorrow." He motioned to himself and plucked at his shirt. A plume of fine red bull dust billowed out from his chest.

"Surprised a city-boy like you would wanna come out here. Sleeping on the ground, covered in dirt and grime. No showering for days."

"I can handle it." I stared him down, annoyed by his assumption that I wouldn't want to get my hands dirty. I may not be a seasoned station hand like they all were, and they might think I was looking at their lives as a getaway, an outback holiday of sorts, but I believed in pulling my weight. I'd be on the four-wheeler the next day. I'd ridden them a few times, so I was familiar enough with the bikes to at least be able to help. In the meantime, serving lunch and dinner, cleaning the dishes, and running favours would have to do. I looked at the cup Craig was holding. Empty. I reluctantly asked, "Want a refill?"

"Nah, mate." He nodded goodbye and wandered over to Ally, bumping into her playfully. I turned away. Watching them made me feel like I was intruding on a private moment. I may have wanted to insert myself into this close-knit group, but I understood that I was an interloper. A temporary visitor out there who'd soon be back in the city. I looked around and sighed from my spot in the sun.

"You okay, Macca?" Waru asked, clapping a firm hand on my shoulder. I'd enjoyed helping him in the stable the day before. He was a good guy. "That's a heavy sigh from a bloke who was so keen to get out here."

"Yeah. Just thinking about how little time I really have here."

"Whatcha got to go home to? Job, girl?"

"Neither. Quit my job when I came here and no, no part-ner." I finished off the last of my coffee and shook out the final drops onto the red dirt at my feet. My forehead creased in thought. Why hadn't Scottie asked me about the permit? Why hadn't he pulled me up? I needed to talk to him about how I could prospect while he had rules about going out alone. I sighed. "But can't exactly stay either." I wanted to though. The first step would be to talk to Scottie about getting out to see the reef. If I found gold, maybe I could stay. The fossicking permit entitled me entry to the land. Usually it was subject to the owner giving permission to enter, except the pastoral lease Pearce Station operated under didn't give them the exclusive rights to the land. That's why Waru and Yindi and their mob could freely walk the property, and apparently, so could I. But knowing that and taking advantage of it when Ma and Nan, Ally, and eve-ryone else had been so hospitable was apparently some-thing I wasn't comfortable with. And then there was Scottie. He played the biggest part in my conundrum. I didn't want to leave him. I didn't want to take advantage, to let him think for a second that in the short time I'd been there, he hadn't come to mean the world to me.

They obviously knew why I was there; the letter I'd posted a month earlier would have arrived well before I did. Problem was I didn't know how to ask, or whether I even needed to, to get out to the coordinates I had.

The break was short and we were packed up ready to move on within half an hour. While Scottie and I were curled up in bed that morning, he'd showed me our heading. The cattle were still relatively close to the home-stead. They kept them rotating through the smaller pad-docks, so it was easier to get feed to them. But at the slow pace we were moving to minimize stress on the animals, we were fighting against time—we still had a lot of ground to cover and darkness fell quickly in the desert. With about five hours of sunlight left, we needed to get the animals to the next bore, or they'd go without water for the night. That would be more stressful on them than moving at the faster pace—something none of us were prepared to do, so we hustled them along.

"Pete, you're with me," Scottie called out. "Wanna take a quick look at the mob from the air?"

"What?" I asked, "From the chopper?"

"Well, we aren't exactly going to grow wings, are we?" He smirked, and I shook my head, jogging over to the bird once I'd tossed the bag into the back of the ute and strapped down the tarp. My heart was beating at a frenetic rate and excitement raced through my veins. Scottie strapped me in, securing the belt around my middle and handing me a set of headphones. "Put the cans on and we'll be right to take off."

I slipped the headphones on as Scottie made his way round the chopper and hopped in his side. A crackle sounded when he slipped the cans on, and his voice came through the speaker in the headphones. "You're not scared of heights, are you?"

"Nope." I grinned at him. "Thanks for taking me up. I can't wait to see what it's like."

Scottie smiled and focussed on the instruments in front of him. Flicking switches and grasping the joystick, he powered up and left my gut on the ground. We rose, and Scottie veered away from the cattle, taking us in the direction we'd come. The chopper swooped in a large arc and he pointed towards the horizon. "I'm takin' you to do a flyover of the ridge. When it rains, it turns into a pond we can swim in, but it's been a while since it's had water in it. We'll go out there one day; it's a nice ride on the horses."

I was about to ask about the ridge, about to open my mouth and say the words. But when it came into view, the words were stolen from my thoughts. Glistening seams of white stood in stark contrast with the red dirt. A ridgeline cut the earth in two, boulders of red rock broken in half at its base. In places, the white rocks were stained red and brown, and in others, they glowed. The quartz crystals reflecting the sun and looking like diamonds lay scattered among the rubble. My breath caught. That was it. It was the reef. The place I'd spent years searching for, trawling through historical records for, learning everything there was to know about Byron. Piecing a picture together of the last months of his life and why the expedition went so wrong. Piecing together the years before that when he was alleged to have discovered the reef. Countless hours spent in basement archives of universities and libraries throughout Australia looking for the key to the mystery. Months of staring at computer screens moving satellite maps an inch at a time to trawl through images that all looked the same, wondering whether the landscape had been obliterated in a hundred years. Flooding, erosion, wind, ground movements—anything could have changed it. But there it was, in front of me. Exactly the same way that Byron had described. Just on the opposite side of the country.

"Pretty spectacular, hey?"

I nodded, then realized he wouldn't be able to see. I turned to him, and the sight before me captured my attention more than the one below. Scottie was beautiful. Up there in the air, in control and keeping us safe. Focussed and a smile on his face. His blue eyes sparkling in the sunlight and his dark hair flecked with grey flopping over his forehead. Suddenly the reef didn't seem so important. It may have drawn me to this place, but it wasn't going to be the thing to keep me there. "Yeah, you are."

"Hmm?" he asked, spotting something in the distance. "Look, eagle."

I followed his line of sight and spotted it in the distance. He was huge. Riding the warmer currents above the land. "Scottie—"

"We should get back."

Frustration and a little bit of fear crept up inside me. I needed time to tell him. To explain my theories. But would I have the courage to actually tell him now that I had so much more to lose? "Yeah. Yeah, we've got a fair ways to go before tonight, haven't we?" He nodded in response, and I placed my hand on his leg. "This okay?"

"Always." His smile made my breath catch and I never wanted that moment to end. I was falling for him. Maybe I already had.

By the time we landed, I'd taken my hand away, and we were back to being friends—acquaintances as far as everyone else was concerned. "Scottie," I said just as he was about to take the headphones off. "Thank you."

"You're very welcome." He reached across me, his fingertips grazing my chest as he unbuckled my seat belt.

"I really wish I could kiss you right now," I breathed. He didn't answer me, but he didn't need to. His lips tilted up in the tiniest of smiles, and his eyes sparkled, full of something that looked a whole lot like affection.

The rotor blades had stopped spinning by the time we got out and ran back over to where Jono was waiting for us. He and Scottie had a quick word, and Jono clapped him on the shoulder before Scottie came around to the ute. The others had already moved off and I watched the dust being thrown up in the distance from the mob. Scottie waited for Jono to take off, the other man tilting his head in a silent salute as he flew away. He turned to me then and grasped my chin, tugging me towards him. I went willingly, wishing that there wasn't a centre console between the seats, and kissed him. It was only a brush of our lips, but it was everything. He pulled away and I touched my lips, the feel of his still on mine. I was sure I looked kiss drunk. I certainly felt it. My smile was shy, and I didn't even mind the flush that stole over my face when he hummed. Scottie brushed his thumb over my cheeks and grinned at me, planting another hard kiss on me.

"We've got to go. Gonna be late to the party." He pushed the ute into gear, and we shot off, bouncing over the landscape as we caught up to the mob ahead of us. Laughing together, we swung in, slipping between the brothers as they kept the cows on the track towards home.

Yeah, home.

The fire blazed, warming the chill in the air. We had our canvas swags rolled out around it, a billy of tea boiling on a metal hook we had hanging above it. "Yeah, it was brilliant," I told Sam. "Scottie took us up and out to the south west—"

"Over to the ridge," Scottie added from next to me. "Figured I'd show Pete some of the rock formations from the sky, given that he's a geologist."

"That what you do, Macca?" Sam asked.

"Yeah, history is my passion, but I've got a degree in geology too. The rock formations are fascinating. The quartz specimens I saw were spectacular. Some of it glittered like diamonds."

"Could there be diamonds there?" Ally asked, curious.

"No, wrong chemical compositions. Typically the indicator minerals are peridotite and eclogite, not quartz. Diamonds form with a low iron content and high magnesium levels. Argyle mine in WA has found diamonds, but there aren't any around here. The dirt has too much iron in it. The glittering is from the silica in the rock."

"How do you know there's no diamonds?" Craig asked.

"The dirt's too red," I answered simply. "It's high in iron, which oxidizes and turns red. It's essentially rust. The quartz there formed from superheated water, likely from below the Great Artesian Basin. Geological surveys of the area show that the landscape was very different during the Cretaceous period. It would have been in the middle of the sea. A hundred million years ago, there would have been dinosaurs swimming around. Covered in icebergs, and the water would have been freezing. There's an island archipelago in the Arctic Ocean off Norway, which scientists think Australia was like. But deep underground, the earth's core would have heated fissures of water and set off a chemical reaction forming the veins of quartz. Geological movements brought it up to the earth's surface. The prehistoric oceans shifted, and Australia dried out, leaving oxidizing sand and the white quartz seams visible to us."

Yindi spoke then. "Us black fellas believe the dreamtime stories."

I nodded in understanding. I'd read the dreamtime stories, usually published as children's books. But I'd never heard one told by an aboriginal person and the scholar in me—the eternal student—was desperate to hear it and learn more. "Will you share a story?"

Waru nodded, and I tracked his gaze round the faces gathered by the fire. I was surprised to see that I wasn't the only person listening intently. "In the beginnin', the earth was flat. There was no life. No trees, no rivers, no plants, no animals." His voice was hypnotic. Slow with an even tempo, Waru had me leaning forward, not wanting to miss a single word. "One day Goorialla, the Rainbow Serpent, woke from his sleep and slithered across the land to find his tribe. From east to west. North to south he searched, carving out gullies and gorges. But he found no one. The earth was silent. Goorialla was tired and lay down. But before he fell asleep, he looked around. The land he saw wasn't the one he'd woken to. It was filled with deep ravines where his body had scored the land. Goorialla decided to create more life and called out to the frogs. They rose out the ground with water in their bellies. He tickled them until the water burst from their mouths and it filled the gullies and gorges, creating the creeks and rivers, the lakes and ponds." Waru looked around again and pointed to a nearby spinifex bush that we could see in the shadow of the flickering firelight. "The grass and trees began to grow and filled the land with the colours of our country. He woke the animals one by one, calling out to each of them now that there was food to eat and water to drink. They lived happily, gathering food and taking it to their burrows to eat. They played in the sand and flew in the skies.

"Goorialla made rules that all the animals needed to obey. He said, 'If you obey, you will be rewarded and turned into humans. If you don't, you'll be punished.' Some of the animals obeyed and were turned into humans. Our peoples were born. Others didn't, and they became the stone that makes the mountains." Waru picked up a handful of the sandy earth and let it fall through his fingers. "We are all connected. Goorialla created the valleys and riverbeds and called forth the water. He made the animals and the humans. He made the mountains." Waru looked to the sky, and my gaze followed. Millions of stars lit it up, a blanket of brilliant pinpricks of light. Its magnificence was humbling.

"Then it started to rain," Waru continued softly. "For many days and nights, it rained. The floods came and the Rainbow Lorikeet brothers, Bil-bil, sought shelter from Goorialla. But the Rainbow Serpent tricked them. He was hungry and said he had no shelter to offer, except in his mouth. The young men climbed in and he snapped his jaws shut, swallowing them.

"Goorialla was ashamed, and afraid the people would realize the Rainbow Lorikeet brothers had gone missing after they went to him for help. He didn't want to be caught. So he hid in the only place he knew he would be safe from them: the sky. But he saw how sad they were after looking for the brothers and never finding them. He tried to make the people happy, turning his body into an arc of colours in the sky. Now, whenever it rains, you can see the Rainbow Serpent there, still saying sorry for takin' the Rainbow Lorikeet brothers."

I was quiet for a moment. Sitting there by the fire, learning an age-old dreamtime story would be a memory I'd recall for years to come. I took in the lessons of tens of thousands of years of history and culture, of pagan religious practices and a unity with the environment. Ethics and morality, life and death, creation, and the need to right wrongs handed down in dreamtime stories through generations of people intrinsically tied to the land. They were one with the earth, not there to conquer it. To rape and pillage it like "modern" man had done.

I knew I'd stumbled upon a new age of grazier with Scottie when we'd spoken that second day. His practices were about as environmentally friendly as cattle droving could be. Everyone on the station was conscious of the impact of their actions and tried to leave as small a footprint on the earth as possible. Knowing the people surrounding him cared just as much about the land as he did warmed me inside. Something told me though, that even if they didn't care, every single one of them would still do exactly as Scottie instructed. I saw it in everything they did—they deferred to his judgement, to his skill. He was a natural born leader, not just their boss. He was someone they would gladly follow.

"Thanks, Waru," Scottie said, breaking the silence. "I've loved that story since I was knee-high to a grasshopper."

"I'm beat," Den said around a yawn. "Need to hit the sack." There were nods from all around us, our group of eight slowly moving into our swags and lying down. I was closest to Scottie; he'd laid his out next to mine, lying parallel to the fire. I lay on my side facing him, watching as he struggled to stay awake.

"Night," he whispered to me as his eyes fluttered closed.

"Sweet dreams," I mouthed to him, knowing he wouldn't hear. I rolled onto my back and looked up, marvelling at the beauty of the stars blanketing the sky. The flat landscape made for a spectacular backdrop to the night sky, lit like a million candles flickering in the breeze. The nearly full moon cast a silvery glow along the landscape. The noises of the night accompanied the crackle of the fire and the soft snores of the hands who'd already fallen asleep. I didn't want the evening to end. I wanted to imprint this feeling, these people and this place on my psyche. I didn't ever want to leave. I wanted to live this life forever. Being in the desert was like coming home. Like finding a missing piece of myself. It wasn't just Scottie either. It was magical. The landscape, the freedom, the hard work, and tough living. The chill in the air and the lowing moos of the mob. It wasn't until I got here that I realized everything I'd done in my life had been leading me to this precise point in time. To this precise place. It was as if I'd been called here, and under this Southern Cross sky, I made a vow to do whatever I could to stay.

With one last look at the glittering sky, and a smile on my lips for what was to come the next day, I closed my eyes, letting sleep claim me quickly.

It was lunchtime the next day when we stopped for a break. Jono landed the chopper a few hundred metres away from where we had the cattle resting. He'd refuelled at the homestead and collected the stew Ma had made, bringing it to us still steaming. The chunks of beef and potatoes in the spicy tomato sauce with fresh damper hit the spot.

I was filthy; the red dust the cows and four-wheelers had kicked up covered me from head to toe. But I loved every minute of it. I was the one whooping from the motorbikes like a yobbo as we herded the cattle along the trail we were cutting through the outback. My experience on a motorbike was limited to the streets and the odd trail ride I'd ridden through the bush closer to home, but I was experienced enough to handle the four-wheelers no problem. They'd all been worried at first, until I showed them that I wasn't talking out of my arse when I said I could ride.

Scottie had been laughing at me all day. The others were convinced I was crazy, but truth was, I was having a blast. Never in a million years would I have thought that my favourite experience in the world would have been herding these beasts down dry, dusty plains under the pale autumn sun five hundred Ks past the middle of nowhere. But then again, nothing about loving this place surprised me—or perhaps everything did, and that's why I'd fallen so hard.

Putting my lunch dish in the plastic bin Jono was taking back to the chopper, I topped up my mug of coffee from the thermos and went to stand with Ally by the horses. "Can I help?" I asked.

"Just checking them over. Making sure they're right for another go."

I petted Nutella, running my hand down her neck then her legs. There was a bur from a prickle bush on one of them, and I reached down, plucking it out of the short hairs on her legs. 'Tella shook her head and nudged me as if saying thank you for pulling it away. "Got something?" Ally asked.

"Just a husk or something. Didn't want it sticking into her."

"Thanks," she said brightly, then motioned in a wide arc with her hand. "You're loving it, aren't you?"

"Totally." I grinned. "Best day of my life."

"It's good you're settling in. You're good for him." Her words were soft enough that there was no way anyone could hear us talking, but I still stiffened, looking around in a panic.

"Scottie's become a good friend," I hedged.

When she laughed, I paled. "Unless I'm reading you completely wrong, you're crushing on him. The looks, the smiles, spending your day glued to his hip. I dunno how he'd handle it if he found out that you're sweet for him, but he's kinda clueless anyway, so you should be safe." I swallowed around the lump in my throat and tried to school my expression. It was a little hard to do when I was practically hyperventilating. "Hey," she murmured, resting a hand on my forearm. "I'm not gonna tell anyone. Your secret's safe with me."

"Yeah, um..." I had no idea what to say to her. Did I try to deny it? Did I agree? What the hell would Scottie want? But then it wasn't really about him either. "Have I been that obvious?"

"Only to someone who's not used to seeing new people round."

"Oh great, so everyone." My sarcasm was immediate, but the very thought of anyone else knowing scared the shit out of me. What if the others didn't particularly like the way I swung?

"Don't worry about the rest of them. It'd never even cross their minds that you're gay. Hero worshipping Scottie maybe, but they'll never think you're attracted to him." She smiled at me, a genuine, beautiful smile. "For the record, it makes no difference to me. You're a youngin', but you fit in here; that's what's important."

"Thanks, Ally. I appreciate you saying that."

"All good here?" Craig asked, his big arms crossed over his chest and a scowl on his face.

"Yeah, mate." Ally breezed by him, plucking her water bottle from the saddlebag and taking a swig.

"You, ah... did good out there. For a city boy." He kicked a stone, never so much as glancing my way as he mumbled his praise.

I huffed out a laugh and shook my head. I wanted to tell him to go stuff himself—his comment the day before was still pissing me off—but I didn't. Biting my tongue, I replied, "Yeah, thanks."

It wasn't long before we'd started the cattle moving again. Jono had gone to double-check the far edges of the paddock to bring any stragglers down to us. The others on horseback, motorbikes, and in the ute, together with the dogs, were looking after the mob, keeping them on track. Scottie and I had ridden ahead, opening the gate for the cattle to flow through to the next paddock, then doubled back to shut off the other remaining bore. It was just the two of us again, out there in the wide-open landscape. The desert surrounded us, the cool air buffeting our faces as we sped over the flat plains.

I spotted the windmill in the distance and smiled as I saw it turning. It was such a perfect representation of the station, the country. Scottie headed straight there, our four-wheelers bumping and bouncing over the terrain. I kept a lookout for snakes, but Scottie had told me that morning they could feel the vibration from the bikes, so they'd be long gone. Thankfully. The last thing I wanted was another run-in with a snake. Didn't matter whether it was a king brown, a red belly black, or a taipan; all of them were deadly.

When we pulled up, I gingerly hopped off the bike and stretched out my stiff muscles. I didn't think I'd ever spent so much time in a single day riding, and I was definitely feeling it, but I was having too much fun to stop. And even if I wasn't, I couldn't just pull over. I'd risk getting separated and lost out here.

I turned my face in the direction of the rotors so I could feel the breeze on my skin, when I realized there wasn't even a breath of wind in the air. *How is it spinning?* I checked the windmill again and sure enough, it was turning slowly. Following the pipes down its centre, I saw the point where the bore delved deep into the ground. Perpendicular to that ran another long pipe. Water trickled from it into a large round tank, low enough that the cattle could drink from it. Scottie went over to the windmill and scaled it, pulling himself up with an ease that spoke of just how strong he was. Already a good storey in the air, he barely paused on his ascent. Once he reached a couple of feet from the precarious point, he looked over the spinning blades and the central mechanism, checking them. He snaked his hand down and adjusted something, making the blades slow and eventually stop rotating. He climbed down, wiped greasy hands on his faded jeans and started to check over the pipes. I looked around for the first time, noticing the solar panel protected by a fence. "So, solar powered if there's no wind?"

"Yep." Scottie smiled and pointed to the panels tilted to face the sky. "The panels power a rotary motor to spin the blades. The windmill then generates enough energy to run the centrifugal pump, which draws the water up from the Basin. We've got it controlled, so it only pumps at a trickle— that way there's no overflow from the tank."

"What happens if there isn't enough water for the cattle?" I leaned against the tower and adjusted my hat so I could see Scottie without the glare of the sun blinding me.

"We have monitoring collars on select cattle. From them, I can get a picture of where the mob is on the station at any one time on my phone." He motioned to the open tank and I followed him when he started walking there. "We've got a sensor in the pump so we know how much water we're bringing up and we jerry-rigged an ultrasonic sensor for the troughs—" He motioned to a piece of aluminium pipe submerged in the water. "—to tell us the water level. The probe's connected to a chip that has something like a GPS system in it. I can see what the depth of each tank is and how much it's changed over a period of time. We know, on average, how much each of the cattle drinks in a day and so we can guess whether we'll have enough. We can come out and adjust the flow to fill it up or they'll just move onto the next bore."

"So, no easy click of a button to adjust it then?" I teased. In truth, I was in awe of him. It was an ingenious solution to a problem that would have been hugely inconvenient to monitor. Hours of driving just to do a five-minute check, if that. Having water being pumped out and spilling onto the ground would have been especially wasteful if there weren't any cattle around too.

"Nah, but it's something I've had Bob from the co-op looking at for me for a while. He's been talking to the CSIRO about it and seeing if there was something we could adapt." On top of the pipe were a couple of taps. Scottie turned them, cutting off the trickle of water into the tanks. "Is that it?"

"Yep, we're all done with this one. But we've got a few minutes before we need to go." He stalked towards me and pinned me up against the A-frame support for the pipe. Lifting my hands above my head, he held my wrists in place while he pressed his hard body into mine. Ghosting his lips over mine, he nudged my nose with his and let out a low growly-hum. I was sure it was part I-want-to-devour-you and part this-feels-amazing. I was in his arms with his warmth touching every part of me, and yet, I still wanted to get closer. I wanted him wrapped around me, inside me, all over me. He felt like home. Like warm sunsets and long walks, like hot chocolate by the fire and lazy days in bed. He was where I wanted to be. Something shifted between us when I stared in his eyes. I could tell he was on the same page as me, that he was just as far gone as me. I wanted to tell him how I felt, that I was falling for him, but I didn't. I didn't want to jinx the relationship budding between us. Instead, I bit it back and leaned in closer, my eyes drifting closed as soft lips touched mine. I let him lead, and he took his time, kissing his fill until I was panting and kiss drunk. He moved his hands, but instead of letting my wrists go, he twined his fingers through mine so we were holding hands and pressed himself harder against me. In the late afternoon, we stood there, kissing in the shadow of a windmill that was generations old, on red dirt full of history and family, and I was sure that when I would look back on that moment decades from then, I'd remember that it was when I'd fallen in love with Scottie Pearce.

# EIGHT

## Scottie

The paw prints I saw as we were taking our time riding back to the mob made me turn the four-wheeler round and get a closer look. Pete stopped beside me and hopped off his bike when I crouched down to inspect the ground. I wasn't sure what made me notice them, or how I'd even seen them in the late afternoon sunshine. We only had about an hour before it'd be dark, so we needed to get a move on, but this was something I couldn't afford to ignore.

I looked closer at the print, as clear as day in the sandy soil. A large pad, flat at the rear and pointed at the front. Four toes closely aligned with two forward and two partially behind. Four claw marks pulled in tight to the pads showing how much higher they sat than a domestic dog's. The print was bigger than my palm—much larger than I'd ever seen. I looked round and spotted another set of tracks, partially obliterated by the four-wheeler's tracks. This one was more like a domestic dog's though. If they were together, it meant a breeding pair—a big dingo and her mate. Damn. Their hearing was better than a human's and it didn't take a genius to work out that they were on the scent trail of the cattle. It was rare that dingoes and feral dogs went for cattle—they were much larger than their usual prey, but I didn't want to risk it. With the mob lowing at night, we could easily have a stampede on our hands if they attacked.

Pete walked away and bent down, holding a hand out to the dirt. When he let out a low whistle, I went to him and my gut sank. The print I was looking at was from another adult dog, easily the same size as the first one. That made at least three of them plus pups. The pups would be a couple of months old given the time of year, and transitioning to meat from their mum's milk.

"Dingo or fox?" Pete asked, looking up at me with fiery green eyes filled with worry.

"Dingo and feral dog. Mum, dad, and a cross-bred pup from last year's litter. If we keep looking, we'll find the smaller pups' tracks too. They're travelling as a pack trying to get some dinner."

"The cows are too big for them, aren't they?"

"Usually, but these are big dogs. They've got to be twenty-five kilos. Dingoes don't usually get much more than twenty." I pulled off my hat and scratched my head, unsure of what to do. When we'd decided to take this station down the route of being more environmentally sustainable, I'd put a halt to the dog culling that Ma and Pops and the generations prior had carried out. I didn't want to be baiting dogs—even feral ones—but I needed to protect the cattle too. And most of all, my people. Dingoes weren't normally trouble—they could find enough tucker without having to attack the cattle, and with the dogs being so close to the chooks at night, that protected them—but this time round, the feral dog worried me. I had a feeling we'd be in for a run-in with them.

"What do we do, Scottie?" He stood then and cupped my face in warm hands. "Tell me and I'll help."

I sighed and closed my eyes, leaning into him. "Can you shoot?" I asked quietly. "I'll be with you the whole time, and I won't let anything happen to you, but I'd feel better if I knew you could shoot."

He visibly swallowed. "Only if you count computer games. My aim's as accurate as it can be from them, but I've never shot an actual gun before."

I knew that'd be his answer—he was a city boy, and most people had nothing to do with guns growing up in Oz—but hearing him say he was virtually defenceless against trained hunters scared the living daylights out of me. I put on a brave face and hoped his bullshit detector wasn't buggered. "That's okay. Won't ever need to anyway." I motioned to the four-wheelers. "Come on, we'd better catch up with the others. Can't slack off too long."

He nodded and I took a step past him, but he grabbed my hand and brought it up to his lips. "Scottie," he said before he kissed my dusty skin. "Thank you for wanting to protect me. First the snake, now dogs."

"S'alright." With my free hand, I fingered the soft skin of his cheek and leaned in closer, grinning when he thought I was gonna kiss him. "This isn't *Call of Duty*, City."

He barked out a laugh and pushed me away, adding, "Good on you, dickhead."

**\*\*\*\*\***

I lay awake looking up at the stars. Pete was right next to me and the others were huddled close to the fire too. The temperature had dropped to freeze-your-nuts-off levels and the fire was stoked high. But that wasn't what was keeping me awake. I could hear howling and more worryingly, barking. I moved my head round, groaning as my neck cracked. Pete shifted and snaked a hand out from his swag, reaching over to me. Squeezing my bicep, he lifted his head and I turned to look at him. "You right?" I saw him mouth silently in the light from the fire.

I nodded, then shook my head when I heard a howl much closer this time. The dogs were stalking the mob and I felt like a sitting duck. The cows were shifting too, mooing and snorting. Stamping their hooves. It was unusual behaviour for the dingoes, but more expected with the feral dog in their midst. Dingoes usually hunted roos, but they'd been on our trail for at least part of the day. We'd followed their tracks—they were using the scrub for cover but trailing the mob and gaining on us. Their strides lengthened as they'd closed in and positioned themselves around us.

We'd called it a day and sat, telling stories about our adventures on the station and others just like it as we were growing up, and listening to another dreamtime story.

And the dogs had watched.

Stalked the mob, picking out the weakest of the cattle.

"The dingoes, yeah?" he murmured.

"Yeah, but the barking is the feral dog. There's a few of them. Can you hear how they're calling to each other from different directions?"

He nodded and asked me a question that had the gears in my mind turning. "If they attack, will they avoid us? I'm guessing they're going for the cattle, but will they keep away from the fire or do they need the light?"

"Huh," I pondered. "They're avoiding us—usually use the cover of darkness for sneak attacks. Maybe if we made some fires round the mob, we could buy a few hours' sleep."

"Or we could split up and build a perimeter of campfires. Rather than moving around all night stoking fires, we could just stay out there with each one."

"Everyone's had a long enough day. To have to do more tonight'd—"

"You two gonna put a lid on it? Some of us wanna get some shut-eye," Dennis grumbled from next to us, my head near his feet.

"Mate, can you not hear the howls?" Pete asked impatiently. "I'd rather keep the mob safe, wouldn't you?"

Waru spoke from across the campfire. "The dingo are hungry. Fires around the cattle might work to ward off a hunt."

"So we do that then," Ally said. I grinned to myself. There I was thinking everyone else was fast asleep, the conversation ending and everyone hunkering down for the night, but instead, we'd all been lying there listening to the pack of wild dogs looking to get a feed out of my mob. I saw

Ally moving, sitting up and putting her jacket back on. Shaking her boots out too. Craig and Sam, lying on either side of her were moving too, and Den sighed and began shuffling around. He must've been doing what the others were—getting dressed again and ready to split up.

I sat up, surveying my hands—my family. "If we're gonna do this, everyone's got to take a gun. Keep it loaded and next to you. You hear anything, see anything, you fire. Anyone hears a shot, get there, quick smart. Our safety is our number one priority, right?"

A chorus of "Yep" and "Yeah" went round the campfire, and I knew there was no point even continuing a debate. The matter had already been settled.

"Right, Waru, Yindi, and Den you stay here." Den made a happy sigh from near my head and snuggled back into his swag. I shook my head and rolled my eyes. Den was a huge help around the station. One of the quiet ones who just did what he had to do. Not the sharpest tool in the shed but one of the hardest working. And above all else—even more than the bottle of Bundy that accompanied him everywhere he went off the station—he loved his sleep. "Craig, Sam, and Ally, you three go to the northern edge of the mob. Take the ute. Radios on and keep an ear out." I paused and smiled at Pete, glad the campfire hid my moment of being kinda shy. "We'll go to the south-western corner on the four-wheelers. Let me grab a couple of logs off the back of the ute so we don't run out of fuel for the fire, and we can go."

It only took a few minutes, and we were off, slowly circling the mob. Pete was right next to me, exactly where I wanted him. Needed him to be. We'd had run-ins with feral dogs before, especially during calving season. But never like this. Then again, it'd never been dry for as long as this either. The tanks housing the water brought up by the bores were high enough that the dingoes would struggle to get a drink from them. I added that to the mental to-do list. Maybe I should cut one of them down so the native wildlife could get easier access to it. Most of the time they got all the water they needed from their food source, but maybe they were just thirsty. God knew I craved a coldie now and then.

The others were heading in the opposite direction, so we were fanned out—a triangle of fires with the cattle in the middle. I kept an eye on the others, Waru, Yindi, and Den's fire anchoring us and the bouncing headlights of the ute as Craig, Sam, and Ally wound their way north. Finally, we reached the end of the mob, and I kept going for a bit longer, separating us to give us all a little room. The last thing I wanted was to end up sleeping between wandering cows.

"You wanna lay out the swags while I get the fire started?" I asked Pete after he'd turned the key, killing the engine of the four-wheeler.

"Yeah, no worries."

I set to work, kindling the fire and building it up so when the twigs burned through, it'd be hot enough to catch the logs. I waited, stoking it and watching the fire catch the bark of the thicker logs. When I turned around and saw Pete, he had the swags zipped together, forming a double bed, and the handgun laid off to the side of him within reach but not too close either. Resting his head on his makeshift pillow— his duffel—wearing a jumper with the swag pulled nearly to his neck, he looked sexy and adorable all at the same time.

"Get in here," he ordered, his voice taking on a rasp that I felt down to my bones. The semi I'd been sporting all day from pushing him up against the windmill came roaring back, and I trailed my eyes down the length of the swag, picturing the beautiful body I'd had naked in my room two days earlier. I kept going, seeing movement below his waist. The unmistakeable up-down motion of him jacking himself. I swallowed, and my arsehole clenched, wanting him inside me again.

I stripped in record time, yanking my boots off and tossing them down carelessly. My jeans and undies went next, but not even the shock of cold air against my nuts cooled me down when I saw the heat in Pete's eyes. I dropped my heavy coat and crawled into the swag in just my flannie and undershirt. I hesitated just for a moment before he cocked an eyebrow at me, and I crawled into his arms. Straddling him, I groaned when my cock lined up with his and he pulled me down, crashing his lips against mine. We were all tongues and teeth and hot breaths on a cold night. I needed skin on skin. Needed to feel the swell of muscle against mine as I rutted on him. Friction, heat, and a zing so strong it took my breath away, had me close to the edge far too soon. I pulled back and shoved my hands under his shirt, pushing it up as I slithered down his body, brushing my lips against his throat. His nipples, pink and pebbled against the cold called to me. Swiping my tongue over them, I smiled as he arched into me and moaned when he threaded his fingers into my hair and tugged hard on the strands as I bit into the soft flesh. His choppy breaths and his stuttering hips told me how much he needed me. It was heady. A turn on like nothing else.

"Scottie," he breathed. My name on his lips sounded like a prayer, and I closed my eyes and ran my hands down his sides. I wrapped my hands round his hips, pressing my thumbs into the sensitive spot he had there and licked a trail up his cock. He cried out, on edge already and I nudged his balls with my nose, licking him again and massaging his hips. That was all it took for him to shout out, cum spurting from his tip onto his flat belly. I licked him clean, tasting his essence and continued up his chest, his throat and finally kissing his lips. I expected him to be boneless, but he held me tight against him, with a hand wrapped round my nape.

I was as hard as a fence post, and I gripped my cock with my callused hand and gave it a squeeze, hoping I wouldn't go off like a geyser, but knowing I wasn't far off after watching Pete come so hard. He batted my hand away and said the words that nearly sent me over the edge. "Need you inside me, Scottie. I've been hard all fuckin' day and seeing you tonight...." He moaned and arched his neck, begging me to leave my mark. I did, sucking him hard as I ground down on him. He was still stiff; his first orgasm must've barely taken off the edge.

"You'll be too sore tomorrow. I can make you come again, but—"

"No, please," he begged. "I need you." He was already pulling the rubbers and lube out of his bag. Who was I to argue? He knew what he wanted—needed—and I sure as hell wasn't going to deny him. Not when I needed him too. I swiped the supplies and tapped his hip.

"Roll over. Lemmie prep you at least." He bit down on his lip and his eyelids fluttered closed. It was the sexiest sight I'd seen. Before he rolled, he tugged his jumper off his shoulders and stuffed it down on the empty side of the swag. Him naked before me was too much to resist, and I did the same, tugging up the swag so we were kinda covered. Pete scooted round when I lifted my weight off him, and he presented his arse to me. I couldn't help linin' up my cock between the two thick hairy globes and watching it slide along his crack as I rocked. His arse, framed by my legs, was a picture of perfection. Absolutely biteable. I squeezed the lube on my fingers and pressed against him, first softening his muscle, then entering him with one, then two fingers. Silken heat surrounded me, tight and welcoming. The arch in his back, the straining of his legs made me want to sink into him with a desperation I'd never come close to feeling before. And the noises he made. God damn, they were sexy. Deep rumbly curses and breathy moans. He shuddered and rocked against me, trying to take more. He was ready, but if I got inside him now, I'd last all of a second.

"Pete," I moaned, kissing his neck and shoulder and pressing my body against his, slowly rolling my hips and grinding on him. He'd laid bites all over my shoulders, leaving little bruises on me, and I loved seeing evidence he'd been there. That he'd marked me. It let me think for a minute I was his. It was stupid, wanting that, but those little marks told me he wanted me, even just until he left. I didn't want to think about him leaving—it was a hell of a boner killer. I'd face being alone again soon enough. But until then, I was planning on enjoying every minute of him. Giving him everything he needed. From the pained groan and full-body shudder he made every time I pressed down, dragging my dick along his crack, what he needed was me inside him.

I sheathed up, slathered some slick onto my cock and grasped his hips, tilting them until I had the right angle. I held a handful of arse cheek in each hand and pulled them apart, so I could line up and slide home. And that's exactly what I did. I sucked in a breath at the same time as Pete when I breached him. That tight ring of muscle clamped round my cockhead, and it was like my first peek at Nirvana. Hot and tight, but it wasn't just that I had a warm body underneath me, welcoming me. It was all him. He pushed back as I got a hold of my orgasm and clamped that bugger down until I was good and ready for it. There was no way I was coming before him. Then I slid forward and rocked slow and steady until we were both on the edge. With the fire crackling beside us, the twinkling star-filled sky above us and the red dirt of the outback below our swag, we were cocooned in a bubble of intimacy I never wanted to escape from. Sweat dripped from my brow and our breaths misted the air before us. The heat of our connection chased away the cold air. I laced our fingers together and buried my face into his nape, licking and kissing his salty skin.

"Scottie," he gasped.

"Whadya need, babe?" I mumbled into his throat, pressing harder into him. Deeper.

His channel fluttered as it tightened round my dick before he cried out and thrust his hips then pushed back against me. I bit down on the fleshy part of his shoulder, trying to hold onto my last shred of sanity before I lost it and pounded him into the dirt, taking what my cock desperately wanted me to do. He turned pliable in my arms as the last of his orgasm left his body, and I couldn't hold back then. Two more deep thrusts and I was shouting into the dark of the night, sending a startled ripple through the cattle lowing nearby.

The radio crackled to life barely a second later; I was still slumped on top of Pete trying to drag air into my lungs and riding a high from the rush. "Yo, Scottie! You blokes right, mate? Out."

I reached out for the radio, swiping at it, but missed. My coordination was all over the shop. Pete chuckled, rolling me off him and picked it up. "Yeah, mate. We're fine. Scottie kicked his toe, getting something from the four-wheeler. Out."

"Serves him right for walking round in bare feet. Dickhead."

"That's your boss you're calling a dickhead, mate," I ground out as I slid the rubber off my sensitive cock and tied it off. It wasn't gonna be the easiest rubbish to dispose of. Apart from the odd container of long-life milk, we really didn't have much by way of rubbish, but there was no chance I was tossing it.

Pete dropped the radio and slid back up to me, pulling me into the wet patch on the swag. "This should be your side," I mumbled against his lips as we curled up together. "We need to get some clothes on or we'll bloody freeze tonight."

"Mmm," he agreed, snuggling into me. I reached out, searching for our clothes shoved down in the swag. I found something and handed it to him, looking for more. As awkward as all hell, we managed to get half-dressed and ended up giving up, content to use each other for body warmth. Socks on, Pete with a jumper and me in a flanny on our top halves and our trackies buried down somewhere near our feet, we wound our legs round each other and used Pete's duffel bag as a pillow. I fingered the hairs on his cheek and sighed happily as he brushed a piece of my too-long hair off my face and leaned in to kiss me. "Night, Scottie."

"Sweet dreams, Pete." I didn't want to close my eyes. But it wasn't the view of the night sky I was looking at. I didn't want to miss a minute of being with the man in my arms. I should have held my heart back—kept it on a bloody leash. I should've just kept it physical, but there was no way with him. He was only with me for a moment in time, but it'd been long enough already for me to fall in love with him. I knew when I was an old man, I'd look back fondly on Pete as the one I loved in spite of his leaving being inevitable. We were already running out of time—I was literally counting down to the date on the Airbnb booking for the guesthouse. It was going to destroy me when he left, the tatters of my shredded heart would reach the breadth of the station. But I'd have to suck it up and keep going. He was my chance at happiness. My shot. And I was okay with that. At least I'd have to be.

Nothing out here was permanent except the landscape itself. The blue sky, the red dirt, the steely blue-grey of the vegetation, the harshness. It all remained constant, even as the seasons changed before our eyes. My family had lived on Pearce Station for generations, and every one of us had faced challenges. I was no different. I had my opportunity now to live every moment together like it was our last. To relish every second with him and store it away on long lonely nights. Every time I closed my eyes in my room, I'd see him. Every time I slept rough on the land doing the mustering, I'd think back to this precise minute when he was curled up and falling asleep in my arms. I had to take solace that I had him now. That even if he wasn't gonna be here forever, I had him for a short while. Maybe that was how it was supposed to be for Ma and me. She'd loved Dad something fierce, and even as a teenager I could see how much she was hurting. But she kept going. She kept running the station and looking after everyone. The sadness still haunted her sometimes. But she hid it better these days. The loneliness only popped up at times, and never when she thought I was looking. I recognized it in her though, like it was a kindred spirit. Maybe that familiarity spoke of what was in store for my life. One-night stands whenever I travelled into Brissie for the Ekka and Sydney for the Royal Easter Show. I'd been satisfied with that BP—before Pete. But after him... well, being a practicing monk out in the desert wasn't too much of a stretch.

"Sleep, Scottie," Pete mumbled. "Gears turning."

I smiled into the darkness, lit only by the fire and the moon now high in the sky, and buried my face in his hair. I didn't want to get all maudlin; I had plenty of time for that later. Now, I held him close and realized that he was the only man I'd ever slept with. It was kind of fitting it was him. His breathing was deep and slow, and he tightened his grip on me as if he was coming to the same realization. But his little snore as he moved told me he was just talking in his sleep.

"I think I love you, Pete McKenzie," I whispered. "I really think I do."

Closing my eyes, I held him tight, trying to feel rather than think, and slowly, sleep took me.

We'd been at it for days, and although we'd walked the cattle slowly, trying not to stress them, I was grateful we were on the home stretch. I could see the reflection off the corrugated iron roof of the sheds winking in the distance. Pete and I were trailing the mob, letting the others on horseback get in first. As much as I couldn't wait to sleep in a bed again, the thought of doing it without Pete made me want to stay out in the paddocks forever. When he'd asked me if we could bring up the rear of the mob, I could've kissed him right then and there. It gave us an extra two hours or so on the others, and even though we were on four-wheelers and couldn't exactly talk or even get anywhere near each other, seeing him there puttering along next to me and keeping his side of the mob in line was enough.

The afternoon sun glinted, almost blindingly bright. Pulling into the big shed was a relief. It was good to get off the four-wheelers and stretch, to shake out our weary muscles. It was just as good to get out of the sun into the cool of the shed. We'd made good time that day, operating like a well-oiled machine. By the time I latched the door on the shed, Ally and the boys had begun the arduous task of sorting the herd. Mating season was just ending, so we'd be separating the bulls and weaned bull calves from their mums and the heifers. Some we'd keep and we'd be selling the others, so we had a lotta sorting to do in the next couple of days until the trucks arrived. We'd usually do it all again in late spring, readying the cows for calving season, but this time we were keeping them in the close paddocks. The desert was so different then. I looked across to Pete and wished just a little that he'd still be with me. As much as I wanted it, it'd never happen though. I bit back my sigh and let out a groan instead when I rubbed my lower back.

"I mistakenly thought that'd be it when we got back. We've got hours of work ahead of us, don't we?" It was a question, but it wasn't really.

I smiled shyly at him and nudged him with my shoulder, before stuffing my hands in my pockets. The heat crept up my face and I looked away before he could laugh. "You don't have to help. You know that, don't you?"

"I know." He clapped a hand on my shoulder and squeezed, his hand lingering there. "But I want to."

"Scottie, a word in private," Ma called from the house. I missed his touch as soon as Pete dropped his hand away.

"No worries, Ma." Turning to Pete, I grinned. "Gimme a sec."

I jogged over towards the house, but I wasn't met with a smile. "What's up, Ma?" I asked as I took the steps two at a time.

She thrust a piece of paper into my hand. "This came in the mail. Your new mate isn't here for a holiday." A sinking feeling echoed through my body when I looked at the form. Neatly typed, it was headed up "Entry notice for private land." The words swam on the page, and I felt lightheaded as I looked over the information, trying to take it in without blowing a gasket or crying like a baby. It was clear as day though. He was exercising his right as the holder of some kind of mining permit to enter our land—my home—and dig it up. Destroy all the hard work we'd put in to make it sustainable. He wanted to make a mess of my station, drain the Basin for wash plants, kill off our wildlife's habitat and damage my family's livelihood beyond recognition just so he could pull minerals out of the ground. He was trying to take away everything we'd worked for, and I'd be buggered if I'd let him do it. If he thought we'd let him do it without a fight, he had another thing coming.

Anger settled over me like a shroud, black as the crows I'd see landing on a carcass. Pete was no sweet, baby-faced city boy wanting a country adventure. He was no historian here to connect with the land. He was a miner looking to get close to us so we'd let our guard down and he'd be able to take what he wanted. He'd used us. Our hospitality. He'd used me. My body. I'd let him touch me and love on me. I'd thought I'd fallen for him. What a crock of shit. My heart cracked open, jagged shards lodging in my chest and making me bleed. The wound cut deep. He'd taken something I'd held precious and used and abused it, and me. My thoughts the night before—of growing old looking back fondly on his time here—disappeared. I'd look back on him with regret. I'd feel the betrayal. I'd feel dirty and cheap and stupid for a long, long time. There wouldn't ever be any soft smiles or happy feels from thoughts of that arsehole.

I didn't even realize I was on the move until my boots hit the red dust. Striding towards Pete, I held up the paper and gritted my teeth, wanting to punch the living daylights out of him. Wanting to hurt him as much as he'd destroyed me. "What the fuck is this?" I seethed through my clenched jaw. I got close enough that I could see the flecks of emerald, bottle green and gold in his eyes. They'd been soft and sexy the night before, but today they were wide, as if he was alarmed. Bumping my chest against his, I pushed at him before bringing my hands up and shoving hard at his chest. He stumbled back, tripping over his feet, and landed on his arse in the dust. Shock lit his features, his startled gaze wide-eyed and his mouth popping open in an O. But when his eyes flicked to the paper I was still holding, that shock turned to recognition.

"Scottie, I can explain," he started, getting a hand under himself to push up from the ground. I held up my own, not wanting to hear it. Whatever he thought was a good enough reason, wasn't. It'd never change the betrayal he'd committed by coming here and inserting himself into our world with an ulterior motive. It was all my fault though—I had to admit that. It was my fault he'd seen so much. My fault he'd been so readily accepted by Ally, Waru, and Yindy and the others. I was there to protect them and their land, and I'd failed. I'd let a man onto our property who wanted nothing less than to mine the site and strip everything of worth off it. I'd invited him to stay, when I should have kicked his sorry arse to the kerb that first afternoon when he said he hadn't had any experience on a station. But if I'd done that then, I wouldn't have experienced any time with him. It'd been special to me, even if he'd just been using me. But I couldn't think that. My anger was already too mixed in with the hurt. Disappointment and heartbreak weighed on me, but I held my head high. I had to. My family was relying on me to provide for them rather than breaking down and crying.

Pete's hand slipped and he fell back onto his elbow, dust covering his clothes, and the bright light in his eyes dimming. Gritting my teeth against the pain blooming in my heart from the upset in his expression, I spat out, "I don't give a rat's arse what your piss weak excuse is. You come on my property, you eat my food, you get all close to me and my family to what? Use us? Destroy everything we've worked for? Get the fuck off my property and don't come back."

"Scottie, please." He reached out for me, but I stepped back, looming over him as he tried. But being out of his reach was a good thing. If he did, I'd snap, and I couldn't be sure what my reaction would be.

"You've got ten minutes. Pack your shit." I turned and strode away from him. I couldn't look at him anymore. Couldn't bear to see his face, to look at those lips I'd kissed. Ally skidded to a halt at my side, and the confusion on her face had me thrusting the paper into her hands as Craig and Sam vaulted the fence to check out what had happened. I walked past them and went straight into the stockyard, intending to lose myself in my work. Or maybe hiding out until everything no longer reminded me of him. I needed to get back to sorting anyways. As much as I wanted to wallow and lick my wounds, the fact was that I had a job to do. And my cattle were more important than my bruised heart right at that moment.

I had plenty of time to fall apart later.

# NINE

## Pete

What had I done? The look on his face would haunt me until my dying day. Pain and anger. Betrayal. It killed me knowing I'd put that there. He'd welcomed me into his home and into his family. He'd given me a piece of himself that I knew he didn't readily give away. He was practically a monk, yet he'd opened up to me. He'd placed his trust in me, and what had I done in return? I'd betrayed him. And in the process, I'd destroyed any possibility of us being an "us," all because I didn't tell him the real reason for me being there. I'd let him think I was visiting on a holiday—or more accurately living there—like I'd found myself wishing for. Instead of being upfront, I'd assumed he'd received the letter and was okay with me making a booking through Airbnb while I was wanting to fossick on the land. I was insensitive and stupid. I'd heard their dreamtime stories and seen some of the places that held cultural significance to them. The land itself was sacred to Waru and Yindi. To the rest of them; it was their home and their family's legacy. And I'd flounced on in there inserting myself into a close-knit family thinking it was all fine. That I'd go out and strike it rich on the reef and move on in with my new boyfriend living happily ever after.

But the postie hadn't delivered the fossicking permit notice. He hadn't known why I was there until it was too late. Until I'd already irretrievably violated his trust. My whole approach, all my thinking, had been flawed. The mail hadn't been delivered in its usual few days like it was in the cities. I should have realized that. I should have made sure that they'd seen it before I'd made myself at home in their guesthouse and fallen for the most important man on the station.

Half lying in the dirt at his feet, watching the anger roll off him in waves and listening to the seething tone in his voice made me want to kick my own arse. He was anything but okay with me being there, with me prospecting his land. Irony was a bitch, wasn't it? I'd been so obsessed with Byron's gold before, but since I'd arrived, I'd only thought about the reef in passing a few times. I'd been enveloped into a life that had instantly drawn me in and found myself wishing for the impossible. I had no idea about living and working on a station, but I found myself wanting to learn everything. And it wasn't just the insatiable student in me desperate to learn more. I'd discovered a love for the big skies and flat red earth, the fresh air and the trillion stars in the night sky, the slower pace, the animals, and the quiet. And Scottie and his family. It was awfully fast to say I'd fallen in love—a week seemed an impossibility, but there was no way I could deny it. I was in love with Scottie Pearce.

When I reached for him, I'd hoped he saw the real me. The me who'd slid my fingers into his hair and kissed him that morning until we were panting and yearning to slide back into our swag and make love again and again. The me who'd slept curled into him the night before, sated after he'd been inside me, and the same the night before that. I wished he'd seen me. Who I truly was, not the gold-obsessed and willing to stop at nothing man I'd been... a week earlier. I closed my eyes, blowing out a slow breath. Had I really changed that much in a week? I knew in my heart that I had, but it sounded farcical even to me. My actions—or inaction—had broken us. I'd hoped he'd say to hell with it, help me up, and we could talk about it over a cuppa. I'd hoped what we'd built together would hold up, but I was being ridiculous in even assuming that could happen. My whole presence there and everything we had, were erected on a foundation that was as unstable as the shifting desert sands. How could there be any hope for Scottie to reach out and trust me to be honest with him now, when I'd destroyed the very thing that tentative trust had rested on? That our relationship had rested on. It was even too much to expect that he'd let me explain—something I should have done the moment I'd pulled up at the homestead that very first day. But I could still wish for it.

"Scottie, please," I begged, not even knowing how to ask for the mammoth olive branch I was asking him to extend my way.

"You've got ten minutes. Pack your shit." His words were clipped, his tone defensive. They were like a stake being driven through my chest, the pain a physical ache.

Then he turned and walked away.

When he left, my heart cracked open. He left a gaping wound in my chest, not unlike the one I'd been searching for in the landscape. I winced and rubbed my chest. But my pain was deserved. Knives pierced my lungs as I sucked in a breath. If I felt this bad, I could only imagine what he was going through. What I'd put him through. I scrambled up, my sore muscles protesting. But before I could chase after him and beg him to give me a chance to explain, to apologize and set things right, Ally appeared in front of me.

She was still reading the form, now grubby with the same red dirt smeared all over both of us, and it halted me in my tracks. I might as well have been facing the executioner. Lifting her gaze, the anger and disappointment hit me like turbulent rapids. Her eyes hard, her mouth turned down in a frown, she folded it, slipped it into her Drizabone pocket, and shook her head. I thought she'd walk away, that she'd call the others to beat me to a pulp, but instead, she raised her eyebrow and pointed towards the guesthouse. "You heard my brother. You've got ten minutes to pack your shit up and leave."

"Ally—"

"You know what, Macca, just don't. Okay? Get off our station and don't come back." She sighed and stomped up to the guesthouse, going through the door and letting it slam behind her. Taking a fortifying breath, I trudged towards the guesthouse. Each step was like getting closer to the executioner. It was irony at its best that I was the one who'd signed my own death warrant. My boots hit the ground and a puff of fine red dust kicked up. I watched myself walk, detached from my own body, as I rounded the stairs and willed myself to be able to walk up them. Up, up, up, and across the veranda. Standing there, hands on hips, Ally watched me like a hawk from just inside the door. My hand closed around the doorknob and I pulled it open, my movements slow and pained. As if my guilt and heartbreak were manifesting themselves in my sheer inability to force myself through it. But one look at Ally had me moving inside. I dragged out my duffel and dumped my clothes into it from the dresser drawers. With each piece that went in, the hopelessness of my predicament—one that I'd bought entirely on myself—grew.

I zipped up the bag and paused there, my shoulders slumping as the shame of my lie of omission weighed heavily on me. The inside of the guesthouse was a mess, red dust everywhere. It was yet another thing I had to apologize for. But the mess wasn't what prompted my next words. "Ally, I'm sorry."

Her huff had me turning to her. "You've got a lot of apologies to make."

I nodded, knowing she was right.

"You lied to him, to all of us, but Scottie especially doesn't take kindly to that. Fairdinkum, Macca, you completely ballsed it up."

I sucked in an unsteady breath and pressed my fingers into the corners of my eyes. There was nothing I could say in response. She was right. I'd ruined everything. Her tone was cold as she prompted, "He'll be back in a minute to drag you off the property if you don't high tail it out of here."

"He's really angry, isn't he?" I asked quietly, knowing the answer already.

Her laugh held no humour. "I don't think I've seen him this pissed before."

"Yeah, that's what I thought." I picked up the bag and dropped it near the door. The only other things I had were laid out on the small table—my laptop and a detailed retelling of Byron's story—and I went over to fetch them.

"Why here, Macca?" she asked. The concern in her voice made me pause. "What makes this land so special that you'd want to tear it up? You'll destroy it."

"I was never going to dig it up with anything more than a trowel, and only a tiny portion of it too. But it doesn't matter now." I shrugged and packed away the laptop.

"I need to know, Macca. This is my home; it's my family's land, and if you're sniffing round, then who else is too? Who are we up against? We can't defend against an Adani or a BHP wanting to come in here."

"I don't think anyone else is looking. I don't think it's even on their radar. Doubt whether it's on *any*one's radar. I'm chasing a myth."

"Huh?" She looked at me, her forehead crinkled and brows furrowed.

"I'm a damn history major. I did a degree in geology because I was obsessed with a story that might never have been true to begin with. I was going to be a real-life Indiana Jones." I handed her the well-loved book. "Here, read that. When you get to the bit where Byron says the reef was west of the Alice, read it as being east."

"*Byron's Gold?* What's this?"

"A legend," I huffed and shook my head. "One that showed me the best possible thing and the worst—me."

"Quit talking in riddles, Macca," she snapped impatiently. "What's Byron's gold?"

"Literally a legend. Byron's reef is Australia's El Dorado." With her disbelieving stare, I tried to explain it to her before she completely ran out of patience with me. "Byron was a storyteller, a paranoid, secretive hustler. Right in the middle of the Great Depression, he bragged about finding a quartz reef laden with gold in the outback. He got in the ear of a union boss and persuaded him to invest thousands of pounds into an expedition that by all accounts failed.

"After trekking across the country in the most godawful conditions, the expedition leader did the only thing he could do—he disbanded the party north-west of Alice Springs. He sent Byron off with a dingo scalper on camelback to see if they could locate the reef and notified the company in Sydney of the unsuccessful outcome. Furious, the expedition's pilot persuaded the union boss to insert him as expedition leader, and to go in search of Byron.

"The history books say that the dingo scalper abandoned Byron and he wandered through the desert and eventually died alone and starving. A body was found with Byron's personal belongings. But back then, there was no DNA identification. No dental records search. He was found with Byron's belongings, so he was identified as Byron. Life was cheap in the outback at that time. With the right motivation—like a gold nugget—it wouldn't have been hard to find a body to stage Byron's death. Without the existence of electronic identities and today's technology, it was difficult to identify with absolute certainty a body that had been exposed to the elements like Byron's had been." I paused for a moment, my next words coming out slowly. I was nervous about telling her. This was where people usually scoffed at me. They'd follow with a look of puzzlement as to why I even know this stuff, and then when I'd tell them the next part, they'd laugh and call me a conspiracy theorist. I knew I'd already blown it here at Pearce Station, but I didn't know if I could listen to Ally's derision without crying like a baby. "I think the history books got it wrong. I think Byron survived." I paused. Waited for Ally to laugh. To react. Instead, she took off her heavy jacket and pulled out a chair, lowering herself into it a little stiffly. I watched her reaction, but her poker face gave nothing away. She wasn't laughing, but she didn't exactly look impressed either. Her mouth in a straight line, her head tilted at an angle, she blinked slowly and waited for me to speak again. I wasn't going to blow my opening. I slid into the chair opposite her and continued.

"Apparently, no one except Byron wanted a plane on the expedition. Cooper, the pilot, and his plane pretty much disappeared at the same time Byron did. What if Bryon hadn't really died? What if he'd faked his death? What if he'd waited until the other expedition members had walked away, then rendezvoused with the pilot again somewhere in the desert? They were documented to have both been at Uluru within a couple of days of each other. What if Byron had lied about the location of the reef to the others but clued Cooper in, then met him at Uluru or somewhere close to it? With a plane like Cooper's, they didn't need much of a runway. They could've landed at the reef, fossicked the gold and stashed whatever the plane could carry, then taken off again. Gold split two ways was better than sharing it with the expedition company and its shareholders. The two of them would've been rich enough to cover their tracks and disappear." I ran my fingers through my hair and tugged on the ends in frustration, groaning. "I've been obsessed with the legend of the reef for years. Searching high and low for something that no one has ever laid eyes on except Byron. No one since has even come close to finding it. But everyone has looked west of Alice Springs. Then I had this idea—maybe the true location was east, not west. Maybe references to Carnarvon in WA were wrong. I thought there was another Carnarvon, and sure enough, there's Carnarvon Gorge in Queensland. It's almost at the same latitude as Carnarvon in WA. I don't think Byron ever meant to mention Carnarvon. He left a breadcrumb and when people started talking about Carnarvon in WA, he didn't correct them. It threw everyone off course. I figured he'd travelled west of Carnarvon Gorge, not east of Carnarvon."

She shifted in her chair, resting her elbows on her knees and took in my rambling, nodding slowly. "And that theory leads you here?"

"Yeah, pretty much. I poured over Google Earth. There's a gully that could match, but it's all speculation." I sighed. "It's pointless speculation now."

Ally rubbed her temples with her fingertips and groaned. "Who finds out about prospecting licences being issued?"

"They're public records. Anyone doing a search can find them." I pursed my lips, wondering where she was going with her questions.

"Who else have you told about your trip here?"

"Everyone knows I'm here, but no one knows the reason why. Mum and Dad think I'm insane, so I don't tell them much of what I'm doing anymore." I shrugged, trying to play off the sting of their criticism. "I actually told them I was coming out here to try to write a paper. Said the same thing to my flatmate. Everyone else thinks I'm here on a holiday."

"What do you want to keep quiet?"

"What? Keep quiet?" I asked, shocked.

"You heard. How much do you want to pretend that this never happened? That you never came out here looking for gold?" Hands crossed over her chest, her gaze hard, she was intimidating. She was a total badarse and I loved her for it.

"Ally, I don't want anything. As far as everyone is concerned, I came out here on holiday. Then I screwed up the best thing that's ever happened to me. That's what's happened here. I'd never betray you guys like that." My shoulders slumped again, and I blew out a breath. "You have no reason to trust me, but I'm begging you to believe me. I... I'll leave." The words tasted like acid on my tongue. Everything in me screamed at me to stay. To fight for him. But how? I knew when I wasn't welcome. And I couldn't exactly profess my undying love for him now—not that I would do it like that—but still... if I was outing myself to his family that'd be one thing, but doing it to him? No way. Been there, done that thanks very much. "I respect Scottie too much to ever say anything."

She studied me long and hard, and the look in her eyes seemed to shift. I wasn't sure whether she was just relenting or if she could see the raw wounds gouged into my chest. "Okay. Come on, get moving. Scottie'll brand you with a bloody iron if you don't."

I nodded, oddly wishing I could wear Scottie's mark on me forever. The hickeys would fade—they already were. In a few days, it'd be like we'd never touched. The ghost of his warm breath on my neck as he kissed along my shoulders and moved inside me would be a memory I'd cherish. It'd have to sustain me; there would be long, lonely nights in my future. I just knew it. And that thought almost brought me to my knees. In the space of a few days—a mere tick in the evolutionary clock compared to the red dirt surrounding us, and the history of a people who'd lived among these trees and under this sky for thousands of years—I'd gone and gotten used to being someone he loved.

I was sure she could see that I was barely holding it together. I was leaving. The weight of it hit me again with so much force, it knocked the air out of my lungs. I looked around one last time and closed my eyes, trying to stop myself from breaking down. I'd barely spent any time in the guesthouse, but that little old Queenslander had been like home. Stupid, I knew, but I could see myself growing old here, Scottie by my side. My whole future flashed before

my eyes, happiness radiating from our every moment together. Now stolen from my grasp by my own stupidity. My
own recklessness. I'd been obsessed with Byron's gold from
the moment I'd heard the story as a young, naïve under-
grad. I'd nearly bombed that first semester's exams because I'd been researching him instead of studying. But I got
my arse into gear, finished up my exams, and headed
straight to the library, devouring everything I could get my
hands on. Then I'd gone searching for more. But it wasn't
enough. It was never enough. I'd been hit with gold fever
and I'd never even seen a speck that was still in its raw form.
I read and absorbed everything I could find on him. Turned
myself into an expert on everything to do with the old pro-
spector over the next three years, but I was no closer to
solving the mystery of the reef. I'd figured the problem was
that I didn't know how to find it. What was I looking for in
the ground? How did I locate a deposit? And that's what I'd
been determined to do—find that reef, discover the gold.
Solve the mystery. Restore Byron's reputation. In doing so I
could give his wives and children their dignity after being
shamed simply for being his relatives. Striking it rich was always secondary—an added bonus, albeit a pretty great one.

So being the diligent student I was, I went back to uni
and struggled my way through another degree, this time in
geology, hating every minute of it. Science wasn't my strong
suit. Neither was maths. But I persisted. Scraped passes in
my subjects and got myself that qualification too. I was
never going to be one of those hard hats on a mining site,

even though I'd majored in extractive geology. Now I knew well enough what to look for. How to read the soil.

I'd searched, hours turning into endless days and weeks, then long months culminating in a couple of years spent squinting at computer screens and pouring over maps. Putting together the puzzle pieces of history with the contours of today and the knowledge gained from my geology degree. I'd convinced myself I was going to find it. And then I'd seen it. A quartz reef. I wasn't sure if it was *the* reef, but it could be. And on that hope, that hunch, I'd packed everything and found myself stepping out of my new-to-me-but-beaten-up old truck and staring at a place so foreign it could have been on the moon. But at the same time, it was like coming home. I'd breathed. Took the clean, dry desert air into my lungs and the weight lifted off my shoulders. My connection with the place had been instant. My future was right there in the blood-red dirt and the biggest blue skies I'd ever seen. I'd wanted to reach out and grasp it with both hands. The moment I'd driven up to the station and passed through the gate marked with two rough-hewn timber posts, and a weathered railway sleeper with Pearce Station burnt into it, I knew where I needed to be. Then I'd seen him. Scottie. The most beguiling man I'd ever laid eyes on. My whole focus changed the moment I saw him. Like a switch flipping, I was no longer chasing a dream. A myth. I was no longer blinded by the search for the reef. It'd been everything to me for so long but in an instant, it became nothing more than a passing interest.

Byron's gold—the stories, my obsession—it all fell by the wayside. For the first time in my life, I reached for something real. Some*one* real. Someone who held my future in his hands, and not the one with me wearing khaki and an Akubra hat crying out in success, or even the one rewriting history and publishing a follow up to the tall tale of *Byron's Gold*. But the one that I'd never even known I could have. The one where I was happy and had a man as wonderful as Scottie to share my life with. Mere days into my trip, we'd been out in the paddocks working side by side, and I knew I never wanted to leave. I wanted those days of living off the land and the nights of making love to last a lifetime. Imagining growing old together, staring up at the brilliance of the stars in the night sky with the red dirt of the outback under our feet didn't feel like a pipedream. I wanted to live and love this man who was honourable and kind. He was the type of man who cared for everyone around him so much that he was prepared to keep a piece of himself hidden forever. But Scottie deserved better. He deserved to shine. To glow as bright as the sun. I'd wanted to give him that.

But I blew my chance. Spectacularly.

I picked up my bags and took a final look at the guesthouse, wishing things had turned out differently. If only I could turn back time…. I shook my head, not even able to go there. Blinking back tears, I sucked in a breath and gripped my chest once more, trying to breathe through the piercing pain. It was too late to save us. I'd shattered any hope of that happening.

I passed through the door, holding it open for Ally as she followed me. What I saw made what little breath I had in my lungs whoosh out of me. Scottie was on horseback, guiding what I knew were the bulls into holding pens. His movements were fluid; he was one with his animal. His blue flannie was unbuttoned and flapping in the breeze, his dark blue Bonds singlet showing underneath. A layer of red dust kicked up by the cattle's hooves hovered in the air as he wheeled and circled them, whistling commands to the dogs. As if he could feel me watching him, Scottie paused, and his gaze met mine. I couldn't see his eyes from under the brim of his Akubra this far away, but the smile I'd been dazzled with before was nowhere to be seen. Instead, his mouth turned down, and he straightened his spine.

"Allyra," he yelled. "Get it done. We need you out here." His words were clipped, angry. But the hurt in them was as clear to me as if I'd been slapped in the face. I'd put it there. It was me that had wounded him. My shoulders sagged, and no matter how hard I tried, I couldn't stop the tears from spilling over.

"I'm sorry," I whispered to Scottie, knowing he wouldn't hear the words. "I never meant to hurt you."

Loading the bags into the covered tray, I slid into the driver seat and started the engine. Like a sucker for punishment, I looked at Scottie once more, but he'd turned away. All I could see was the back of his hat-covered head where I'd nuzzled and kissed as we'd lain together or made love and his broad shoulders and narrow waist. I'd wrapped my arms tight around that waist and been held by those strong arms as he'd cuddled me close. His hands gripping the reins were callused and rough but tender too. His touch could be as light as a feather, and the ghost of it and his lips on my own taunted me as I sat there, my chest constricting and my tears welling over again.

"You dickhead," I muttered, pissed at myself for how bloody stupid I'd been. "Fucked it entirely." Angrily wiping my cheeks with the heel of my hands, I slammed the car into gear, pulling away from the guesthouse in a cloud of fine red dust.

I managed to get about five Ks away before I had to pull over. I couldn't breathe. Couldn't see. Hot tears rolled down my cheeks, and I gasped for breath as I dragged my arse out of my ute. Tripping over my own feet, I stumbled and landed on my knees in the dirt. I splayed my fingers in the fine red dust until it covered them. Unlike the hard-packed earth on the driveway, to the side it was sandy and loose. Dry as a bone. It was warm on the surface but a few inches down, it was cool—a strange thing to notice under the circumstances. It made my reality all the harder to swallow. I knelt there, on my hands and knees in the red dirt, sobbing. I couldn't get the air in my lungs and couldn't stop the tears tracking down my face. My nose was running, the wet leaving streaks on my dirt-stained hands. And still, the heaving sobs wracking my body didn't let up. I'd lost everything: I'd lost Scottie. I pulled my hat off and threw it at the ground in frustration. That stupid hat was so typical of everything I'd done wrong. I'd bought it in the city. Walked into some store in the Sydney CBD and asked for something that'd suit me out west. It was as if I'd thought I could come out here and fit right in. Like I'd become their mate when, really, I was here to throw their lives into chaos. But the joke was on me. I gripped the unwashed strands of my hair and tugged hard. The pain was nothing compared to the gaping wound in my chest that I'd caused with my fuck ups. Empty. That's what I was inside. This vacuum of nothingness except pain. As vast and inescapable as the landscape in front of me. Bleakness. I wanted to rail and shout, to kick something, but what was the point? I was still faced with the same reality and I only had myself to blame.

The strange-sounding deep rolling grunt in the quiet afternoon had me peering through my tear-stained hands. Directly in front of me were two clawed feet as big as dinner plates connected to long, skinny, leathery legs taller than my kneeling form. A thatch of brown feathers and out-stretched wings that were far too small for its round body made it huge and combined with its long neck had the bloody thing standing well over ten feet tall—at least that's what it felt like from down there on the ground. Don't judge, you'd shit yourself if you were faced with that too. It towered over me, its beady eyes assessing me as I swallowed hard and tried to figure out how to not die. Its pointy beak could do some damage, but it was its giant claws I was terrified of. Emus defended themselves by kicking out at a threat—I knew that much—and I didn't want to be any form of threat. I held my breath, not daring to move a muscle. Trying not to flinch at it. Was that even the right thing to do? I hadn't exactly read an instruction book on how not to die by emu. What the hell did it want?

It didn't take long to find out. Taking a step closer, the emu bent down and, never breaking eye contact with me, snatched my hat up by the shiny buckle. Then it was gone. Like poof. One minute it was standing in front of me, probably assessing whether it wanted to gut me after it lifted my hat, and the next it was taking long strides in the opposite direction, running at full pelt. It was across the driveway and over the wire fence in a matter of seconds.

My breath came whooshing out of my lungs, and I slowly pushed to my feet from the dusty ground. I didn't want to be down there again in case the next wild animal I ran into wasn't as satisfied with what they could steal. Because if the locals out here didn't kill you, the wildlife could and probably would. On unsteady legs, I made my way back to the door and slowly sank into the seat. My hands were shaking as much as my knees and I gripped the steering wheel tight to keep me upright.

I had no idea how long I was sitting there, my heart hammering out a staccato beat when Waru gave me another fright of my life. He popped up from nowhere, resting an arm on the door and another on the roof, leaning into the open space. "You right, mate?"

"Oh shit," I stammered as I jumped. "Yeah, nearly got shanked by an emu."

"While you were driving?" He looked at me with obvious confusion, his brows furrowed and lips turned down.

"Nah, I got out. Dropped my hat and it nicked off with it."

"Ah, yeah, mate. Those emus like shiny stuff." He nodded knowingly and the conversation stalled.

After the silence had stretched on a beat too long to be comfortable, I asked, "Come to check up on me, huh? Making sure I left." He shrugged, leaving the question unanswered, but I knew the truth. The question was whether Scottie had asked him to, or whether Waru had decided to check himself. Either way, I was deluding myself if I thought that the answer meant anything more than either one of them wanting me gone for good. "Yeah, righteo then. I'll be off." I paused and added, "Waru, I never meant to hurt anyone. I didn't want to betray your trust. I... I never..."

"Funny way of going about it, Macca." He raised his eyebrows and I took it as my cue to leave. He was right too. Clearly I didn't belong out there. Not only did the people want me to leave, but the bloody native animals were telling me to piss off. I turned the key in the ignition, pulled the door closed after Waru stepped back, eased it into gear and took off with the heaviest of hearts. I was going home. Going back to the city where the apartment and office building lights served as the stars and I didn't have to worry about concrete getting into everything like the red dust out here did. And that thought was the most heartbreaking of all, because I wanted to fit in. I really, really did.

Four hours later and well after the sun had set, I pulled into Longreach. For a country town, the roads were busy. But it wasn't local traffic; it was trucks. Road trains and big semis passed me on the way in, when I'd joined the main highway, but where they were continuing onto their destinations, I had to stop. My muscles were weary from days on the four-wheelers and sleeping rough under the stars. Days that'd live in my memory forever with bittersweetness. Every part of my body ached. Eyes scratchy from the dust, the sun, exhaustion or from crying, I couldn't be sure, but that was nothing compared to the rest of me. All I knew was that I needed a wash and some sleep.

Back in the land of mobile phone reception, I pulled into the closest servo, filled up, and googled the motels in town. The one boasting that it was right next door to the pub answered on the first ring and told me that they had a vacancy for a few nights. I didn't hesitate, driving the last few minutes there, and once I was checked in, I fell into the shower and scrubbed away the filth of my days mustering. My eyes were closing before I'd even dried myself and I stumbled from the tiny stall onto the double bed, falling face first onto it. The bed was covered by a red, gold, and rust-covered spread that was scratchy to the touch, but I barely noticed as I pulled it over me and slept like the dead.

**\*\*\*\*\***

I wasn't sure what time I woke up the next morning, or what woke me, but once I was up, I realized that sleep didn't always fix things. Everything that looked shitty the night before, still looked just as shitty that morning. I groaned and pressed the pillow against my face, muffling my shout of frustration. I had to get the hell out of there. Longreach was like a frontier town. Most people passed through it to get somewhere else. For me, it was the gateway to wonder. An almost childlike enchantment with the desert and a man in it. Now that I'd screwed it up, there was nothing left. Why had I told them I'd be there for a week or two?

Niggling thoughts of Ally's words wouldn't leave me. They kept playing on a loop in my head—who else knew? Who else would they need to fight? I didn't want them to be constantly looking over their shoulders. I'd caused them enough grief. Especially Scottie. I needed to make it right. I needed to make sure that I nipped it in the bud before that worry had a chance to take root. And lying in that bed under the folded scratchy spread, and a lumpy pillow, it hit me. I knew exactly how to fix it.

I dressed and programmed the address for the Department of Natural Resources and Mines into Google. Less than five minutes later, I was walking up the stairs to the government office that looked after mining and prospecting permits for the region.

"Next please." The lady paused as I sat in front of her. "How can I help?"

"Hi, uh, my name's Peter McKenzie. I was granted a pro-specting licence recently over a little area of land a few hours away from here. I've finished up so I figured I'd cancel it."

She took down my details and typed away at the computer. "It's still valid for quite some time. You sure you want to cancel it? You don't plan on going back?"

"There's nothing out there." I paused for a moment as an idea took root. "But could I transfer it? Maybe to the owners? I doubt whether they'll do anything with it, but it can't hurt."

"Yeah, you can absolutely transfer it. Fill out this form, have both parties sign at the bottom and return it here with the fee." I took the paperwork and walked away, disheart-ened. I couldn't pull it off without going back out to the sta-tion, and as much as I wanted to fix it, I didn't want to risk the branding iron I'd been threatened with. Or the bullwhip I'd seen Scottie crack into the air to get the cattle moving.

Unless...

Unless I did something totally illegal and crazy stupid, but something that Scottie might actually appreciate. But could I? Should I? What if I got busted? What was the worst that could happen? I dared not ask that question, because it was probably pretty bad. Like jailtime bad. Was I prepared to risk it? For him, there was only one answer. Yes.

Resolve straightened my spine, and the smile I was hold-ing back split my face. I walked out of the government office and headed straight to the pub for brekkie. Well, lunch—it was well after noon by the time I made it there.

I pushed around the last of my schnitzel, trying to decide whether I should hand deliver the transferred licence or put it in the post again. Maybe I could somehow get in contact with Ally and email her a copy. It was probably the best option—at least I could get confirmation it'd been read. I brought up the station's website looking for direct email addresses but had no luck. Instead, I stumbled over the bio section. There was a photo of Scottie in action, much like what he'd been doing when I'd left. He was on Tilly steering cattle into the holding yards, dust kicking up, and creating a red haze in the air. I saved the image, knowing it was the only one I'd ever have of him. I wanted him more than ever, but I kept on scrolling down to Ally, finding her profile.

When I found her, I laughed. She was kneeling in the dirt, between Craig and Sam laughing. Knife in hand, she was holding down a brown snake as thick as my arm, running the blade down its body. I shuddered. As far as I was concerned, the only good snake was a long-dead one. But it wasn't the picture which held my attention. It was her name: Allyra Pearce. I'd assumed her name was Allison. But I remembered Scottie's words "Allyra, get it done". I hadn't put two and two together then—my emotions were taking a bit of a beating. They weren't any better now, but at least I could focus on what was in front of me. My last few moments at the station were spent using every ounce of my strength to stay upright and do what Scottie demanded and leave. I'd barely had the wherewithal to follow that direction, never mind take much notice of what he'd called his sister. Everything about those moments were imprinted on my memory. The smell of the cattle, the dust, the pain and anger crossing Scottie's features. The betrayal he'd so clearly felt. And the utter ravaging of my heart knowing it was me who'd hurt the man I'd fallen in love with. I closed my eyes and relived those moments, Scottie sitting tall on Tilly, reins in hand and his hat covering his facial features that I knew had hardened when he'd looked at me. The terse tone of his voice as he yelled out to his sister. My chest squeezed and I rubbed the ache that stole my breath, willing myself not to break down again.

I blinked open my eyes and inhaled slowly, trying to focus on the words swimming in front of me. But all I could see was the red dirt and blue sky behind Ally. The knowledge that I'd never see that land again and the people on it broke my heart.

I forced myself to focus. To push through the desire to curl up and cry. Allyra. Her name. That's what I was thinking about. It was a beautiful name, it really was. Exotic and unique. I hadn't heard it before. What was its origin? Another mystery to solve. This one would likely be much easier than Byron's gold.

And one I hopefully couldn't screw up.

But what was even the point? It wasn't like I could stay. The thought of leaving though, of going home seemed like a foreign concept now.... I'd never be the same again after having lived in the outback, even if it was for a short time. Big skies and a land that held so much history and was as red as it was sacred had changed me. I knew I would feel like a fish out of water between the skyscrapers and shadowed streets of Sydney. I hung my head, thinking about what it would have been like for the men on Byron's expedition to go home. There would have been a mix of relief that it was over and shame that they'd all been fooled by a man who was paranoid and secretive at best, and at worst, a crazy bastard. Thousands of pounds were invested in what was ultimately a wild goose chase. I huffed. That tale sounded a lot like my own. Swindled like a fool, placing my blind faith into a legend that'd never been substantiated, wasting years of my life on it and spending hundreds of thousands of dollars that I didn't have. My uni debts were sky-high, and I'd lived like a pauper to save up enough to get a truck and get out here for a few months. All because I was stupid enough to think that that there was more to the fable—a chance of finding the reef and changing history.

Guess I'd never know whether there was more to the myth of gold-laden reef in the red centre.

*The end... for now.*
*Pete and Scottie's story concludes in*
*Outback Treasure II.*

## BOOK TWO OF THE
## PEARCE STATION DUET

**Deception tore them apart, but Pete and Scottie are drawn to each other like a moth to the flame. Trust and friendships are tested in Pete's mission to rewrite the legend of the golden reef before time runs out.**

Scottie Pearce never planned on falling for anyone, especially not the geeky history graduate nearly half his age. He and his lover have unfinished business. But is nature conspiring against them? The desert trying to tear them apart?

When secrets are revealed, who will be left standing?

Outback Treasure II is a blazing inferno, an epic tale of lust and love. But is time running out as these men fight to keep that which they treasure most... their outback treasure.

**Outback Treasure II is a continuation of Pete and Scottie's story. The first book in the Pearce Station duet is Outback Treasure I.**

## ABOUT ANN GRECH

By day Ann Grech lives in the corporate world and can be found sitting behind a desk typing away at reports and papers or lecturing to a room full of students. She graduated with a PhD in 2016 and is now an over-qualified nerd. Glasses, briefcase, high heels and a pencil skirt, she's got the librarian look nailed too. If only they knew! She swears like a sailor, so that's got to be a hint. The other one was "the look" from her tattoo artist when she told him that she wanted her kids initials "B" and "J" tattooed on her foot. It took a second to register that it might be a bad idea.

She's never entirely fit in and loves escaping into a book—whether it's reading or writing one. But she's found her tribe now and loves her MM book world family. She dislikes cooking, but loves eating, can't figure out technology, but is addicted to it, and her guilty pleasure is Byron Bay Cookies. Oh and shoes. And lingerie. And maybe handbags too. Well, if we're being honest, we'd probably have to add her library too given the state of her credit card every month (what can she say, she's a bookworm at heart)!

She also publishes her raunchier short stories under her pen name, Olive Hiscock.

Ann loves chatting to people online, so if you'd like to keep up with what she's got going on:

Join her newsletter: http://anngrech.us8.list-
manage2.com/subscribe?u=0af7475c0791ed8f1466e
7fd9&id=1cee9cdcb6
Like her on Facebook:
https://www.facebook.com/pages/Ann-
Grech/458420227655212
Join her reader group:
https://www.facebook.com/groups/1871698189780
535/
Follow her on Twitter and Instagram:
@anngrechauthor
Follow her on Goodreads:
https://www.goodreads.com/author/show/7536397.
Ann_Grech
Follow her on BookBub:
https://www.bookbub.com/authors/ann-grech
Visit her website (www.anngrech.com) for her
current booklist


She'd love to hear from you directly, too. Please feel
free to e-mail her at ann@anngrech.com or check
out her website www.anngrech.com for updates.

## OTHER BOOKS BY ANN GRECH

---

### UNEXPECTED

*Whiteout (MM)*
*White Noise (MM)*
*Whitewash (MM)*

### MY TRUTH

*All He Needs (MMM)*
*In Safe Arms (MM)*

### GOLD COAST NIGHTS

*Delectable (MMF)*

### MV DREAMCATCHER

*Dance with Me (MM)*

### STANDALONES

*Home For Christmas (MM)*
*The Gift (FMMM - free for newsletter subscribers)*

### M/F TITLES

*One night in Daytona*
*Ink'd*